MAROONED . . .

"What happened? Why did the ship blow up?"

"They blitzed us," Cargraves said savagely. "They bombed us out. If we had been aboard they would have killed us. That's what they meant to do."

"But why?"

"No possible reason. They didn't want us here." He refrained from saying what he felt to be true: that their unknown enemy had failed only temporarily in his intent to kill.

A quick death by high explosives would probably be a blessing compared with what he felt was in store for them: marooned . . . on a dead and airless planet!

Also by Robert A. Heinlein
published by Ballantine Books:

SPACE CADET
RED PLANET
FARMER IN THE SKY
BETWEEN PLANETS
THE ROLLING STONES
STARMAN JONES
THE STAR BEAST
TUNNEL IN THE SKY
TIME FOR THE STARS
CITIZEN OF THE GALAXY
HAVE SPACE SUIT—WILL TRAVEL

Rocket Ship Galileo

Robert A. Heinlein

A Del Rey Book

BALLANTINE BOOKS • NEW YORK

For COLIN, MATT, and BUDDY

A Del Rey Book
Published by Ballantine Books

ISBN 0-345-32743-8

Printed in Canada

First Ballantine Books Edition: August 1977
Seventh Printing: April 1985

Cover art by Darrell Sweet

CONTENTS

I "LET THE ROCKET ROAR"

"Everybody all set?" Young Ross Jenkins glanced nervously at his two chums. "How about your camera, Art? You sure you got the lens cover off this time?"

The three boys were huddled against a thick concrete wall, higher than their heads and about ten feet long. It separated them from a steel stand, anchored to the ground, to which was bolted a black metal shape, a pointed projectile, venomous in appearance and ugly—a rocket. There were fittings on each side to which stub wings might be attached, but the fittings were empty; the creature was chained down for scientific examination.

"How about it, Art?" Ross repeated. The boy addressed straightened up to his full five feet three and faced him.

"Look," Art Mueller answered, "of course I took the cover off—it's on my check-off list. You worry about your rocket—last time it didn't fire at all and I wasted twenty feet of film."

"But you forgot it once—okay, okay, how about your lights?"

For answer Art switched on his spotlights; the beams shot straight up, bounced against highly polished stainless-steel mirrors and brilliantly illuminated the model rocket and the framework which would keep it from taking off during the test. A third boy, Maurice Abrams, peered at the scene through a periscope which allowed them to look over the reinforced concrete wall which shielded them from the rocket test stand.

7

"Pretty as a picture," he announced, excitement in his voice. "Ross—do you really think this fuel mix is what we're looking for?"

Ross shrugged. "I don't know. The lab tests looked good—we'll soon know. All right—places, everybody! Check-off lists—Art?"

"Complete."

"Morrie?"

"Complete."

"And mine's complete. Stand by! I'm going to start the clock. Here goes!" He started checking off the seconds until the rocket was fired. "Minus ten . . . minus nine . . . minus eight . . . minus seven . . . minus six . . . minus five . . . minus four. . . ." Art wet his lips and started his camera. "Minus three! Minus two! Minus one!—*Contact!*"

"*Let it roar!*" Morrie yelled, his voice already drowned by the ear-splitting noise of the escaping rocket gas.

A great plume of black smoke surged out the orifice of the thundering rocket when it was first fired, billowed against an earth ramp set twenty feet behind the rocket test stand and filled the little clearing with choking fumes. Ross shook his head in dissatisfaction at this and made an adjustment in the controls under his hand. The smoke cleared away; through the periscope in front of him he could see the rocket exhaust on the other side of the concrete barricade. The flame had cleared of the wasteful smoke and was almost transparent, save for occasional sparks. He could actually see trees and ground through the jet of flame. The images shimmered and shook but the exhaust gases were smoke-free.

"What does the dynamometer read?" he shouted to Morrie without taking his eyes away from the periscope.

Morrie studied that instrument, rigged to the test stand itself, by means of a pair of opera glasses and his own periscope. "I can't read it!" he shouted. "Yes, I can—wait a minute. Fifty-two—no, make it a hundred and fifty-two; it's second time around. Hunderfiftytwo, fif'three, -four. Ross, you've done it! You've done it! That's more than twice as much thrust as the best we've ever had."

Art looked up from where he was nursing his motion-picture camera. It was a commercial 8-millimeter job, modified by him to permit the use of more film so that every second of the test could be recorded. The modification worked, but was cantankerous and had to be nursed along. "How much more time?" he demanded.

"Seventeen seconds," Ross yelled at him. "Stand by—I'm going to give her the works." He twisted his throttle-monitor valve to the right, wide open.

The rocket responded by raising its voice from a deep-throated roar to a higher pitch with an angry overtone almost out of the audible range. It spoke with snarling menace.

Ross looked up to see Morrie back away from his periscope and climb on a box, opera glasses in hand. "Morrie—get your head down!" The boy did not hear him against the scream of the jet, intent as he was on getting a better view of the rocket.

Ross jumped away from the controls and dived at him, tackling him around the waist and dragging him down behind the safety of the barricade. They hit the ground together rather heavily and struggled there. It was not a real fight; Ross was angry, though not fighting mad, while Morrie was merely surprised. "What's the idea?" he protested, when he caught his breath.

"You crazy idiot!" Ross grunted in his ear. "What were you trying to do? Get your head blown off?"

"But I wasn't—" But Ross was already clambering to his feet and returning to his place at the controls; Morrie's explanation, if any, was lost in the roar of the rocket.

"What goes on?" Art yelled. He had not left his place by his beloved camera, not only from a sense of duty but at least partly from indecision as to which side of the battle he should join.

Ross heard his shout and turned to speak. "This goon," he yelled bitterly, jerking a thumb at Morrie, "tried to——"

Ross's version of the incident was lost; the snarling voice

of the rocket suddenly changed pitch, then lost itself in a bone-shaking explosion. At the same time there was a dazzling flash which would have blinded the boys had they not been protected by the barricade, but which nevertheless picked out every detail of the clearing in the trees with brilliance that numbed the eyes.

They were still blinking at the memory of the ghastly light when billowing clouds of smoke welled up from beyond the barricade, surrounded them, and made them cough.

"Well," Ross said bitterly and looked directly at Morrie, "that's the last of the *Starstruck V*."

"Look, Ross," Morrie protested, his voice sounding shrill in the strange new stillness, "I didn't do it. I was only trying to——"

"I didn't say you did," Ross cut him short. "I know you didn't do it. I had already made my last adjustment. She was on her own and she couldn't take it. Forget it. But keep your head down after this—you darn near lost it. That's what the barricade is *for*."

"But I wasn't going to stick my head up. I was just going to try——"

"Both of you forget it," Art butted in. "So we blew up another one. So what? We'll build another one. Whatever happened, I got it right here in the can." He patted his camera. "Let's take a look at the wreck." He started to head around the end of the barricade.

"Wait a minute," Ross commanded. He took a careful look through his periscope, then announced: "Seems okay. Both fuel chambers are split. There can't be any real danger now. Don't burn yourselves. Come on." They followed him around to the test stand.

The rocket itself was a complete wreck but the test stand was undamaged; it was built to take such punishment. Art turned his attention to the dynamometer which measured the thrust generated by the rocket. "I'll have to recalibrate this," he announced. "The loop isn't hurt, but the dial and the rack-and-pinion are shot."

The other two boys did not answer him; they were busy

with the rocket itself. The combustion chamber was split wide open and it was evident that pieces were missing. "How about it, Ross?" Morrie inquired. "Do you figure it was the metering pump going haywire, or was the soup just too hot for it?"

"Hard to tell," Ross mused absently. "I don't think it was the pump. The pump might jam and refuse to deliver fuel at all, but I don't see how it could deliver too much fuel—unless it reared back and passed a miracle."

"Then it must have been the combustion chamber. The throat is all right. It isn't even pitted—much," he added as he peered at it in the gathering twilight.

"Maybe. Well, let's throw a tarp over it and look it over tomorrow morning. Can't see anything now. Come on, Art."

"Okay. Just a sec while I get my camera." He detached his camera from its bracket and placed it in its carrying case, then helped the other two drag canvas tarpaulins over all the test gear—one for the test stand, one for the barricade with its controls, instruments, and periscopes. Then the three turned away and headed out of the clearing.

The clearing was surrounded by a barbed wire fence, placed there at the insistence of Ross's parents, to whom the land belonged, in order to keep creatures, both four-legged and two-legged, from wandering into the line of fire while the boys were experimenting. The gate in this fence was directly behind the barricade and about fifty feet from it.

They had had no occasion to glance in the direction of the gate since the beginning of the test run—indeed, their attentions had been so heavily on the rocket that anything less than an earthquake would hardly have disturbed them.

Ross and Morrie were a little in front with Art close at their heels, so close that, when they stopped suddenly, he stumbled over them and almost dropped his camera. "Hey, watch where you're going, can't you?" he protested. "Pick up your big feet!"

They did not answer but stood still, staring ahead and at the ground. "What gives?" he went on. "Why the trance? Why do—oh!" He had seen it too. "It" was the body of a

11

large man, crumpled on the ground, half in and half out the gate. There was a bloody wound on his head and blood on the ground.

They all rushed forward together, but it was Morrie who shoved them back and kept them from touching the prone figure. "Take it easy!" he ordered. "Don't touch him. Remember your first aid. That's a head wound. If you touch him, you may kill him."

"But we've got to find out if he's alive," Ross objected.

"I'll find out. Here—give me those." He reached out and appropriated the data sheets of the rocket test run from where they stuck out of Ross's pocket. These he rolled into a tube about an inch in diameter, then cautiously placed it against the back of the still figure, on the left side over the heart. Placing his ear to the other end of the improvised stethoscope he listened. Ross waited breathlessly.

Presently his tense face relaxed into a grin. "His motor is turning over," he announced. "Good and strong. At least we didn't kill him."

" 'We'?"

"Who do you think? How do you think he got this way? Take a look around and you'll probably find the piece of the rocket that konked him." He straightened up. "But never mind that now. Ross, you shag up to your house and call an ambulance. Make it fast! Art and I will wait here with . . . with, uh, him. He may come to and we'll have to keep him quiet."

"Okay." Ross was gone as he spoke.

Art was staring at the unconscious man. Morrie touched him on the arm. "Sit down, kid. No use getting in a sweat. We'll have trouble enough later. Even if this guy isn't hurt much I suppose you realize this about winds up the activities of the Galileo Marching-and-Chowder Society—at least the rocketry-and-loud-noises branch of it."

Art looked unhappy. "I suppose so."

" 'Suppose' nothing. It's certain. Ross's father took a very dim view of the matter the time we blew all the windows out of his basement—not that I blame him. Now we hand

12

him this. Loss of the use of the land is the least we can expect. We'll be lucky not to have handed him a suit for damages too."

Art agreed miserably. "I guess it's back to stamp collecting for us," he assented, but his mind was elsewhere. Law suit. The use of the land did not matter. To be sure the use of the Old Ross Place on the edge of town had been swell for all three of them, what with him and his mother living in back of the store, and Morrie's folks living in a flat, but—*law suit!* Maybe Ross's parents could afford it; but the little store just about kept Art and his mother going, even with the after-school jobs he had had ever since junior high—a law suit would take the store away from them.

His first feeling of frightened sympathy for the wounded man was beginning to be replaced by a feeling of injustice done him. What was the guy doing there anyhow? It wasn't just trespass; the whole area was posted with warning signs.

"Let me have a look at this guy," he said.

"Don't touch him," Morrie warned.

"I won't. Got your pocket flash?" It was becoming quite dark in the clearing.

"Sure. Here . . . catch."

Art took the little flashlight and tried to examine the face of their victim—hard to do, as he was almost face down and the side of his face that was visible was smeared with blood.

Presently Art said in an odd tone of voice, "Morrie—would it hurt anything to wipe some of this blood away?"

"You're dern tootin' it would! You let him be till the doctor comes."

"All right, all right. Anyhow I don't need to—I'm sure anyhow. Morrie, I know who he is."

"You do? Who?"

"He's my uncle."

"Your *uncle!*"

"Yes, my uncle. You know—the one I've told you about. He's my Uncle Don. Doctor Donald Cargraves, my 'Atomic Bomb' uncle."

II A MAN-SIZED CHALLENGE

"At least I'm pretty sure it's my uncle," Art went on. "I could tell for certain if I could see his whole face."

"Don't you know whether or not he's your uncle? After all, a member of your own family——"

"Nope. I haven't seen him since he came through here to see Mother, just after the war. That's been a long time. I was just a kid then. But it looks like him."

"But he doesn't look old enough," Morrie said judiciously. "I should think— Here comes the ambulance!"

It was indeed, with Ross riding with the driver to show him the road and the driver cussing the fact that the road existed mostly in Ross's imagination. They were all too busy for a few minutes, worrying over the stranger as a patient, to be much concerned with his identity as an individual. "Doesn't look too bad," the interne who rode with the ambulance announced. "Nasty scalp wound. Maybe concussion, maybe not. Now over with him—easy!—while I hold his head." When turned face up and lifted into the stretcher, the patient's eyes flickered; he moaned and seemed to try to say something. The doctor leaned over him.

Art caught Morrie's eye and pressed a thumb and forefinger together. There was no longer any doubt as to the man's identity, now that Art had seen his face.

Ross started to climb back in the ambulance but the interne waved him away. "But all of you boys show up in the hospital. We'll have to make out an accident report on this."

14

As soon as the ambulance lumbered away Art told Ross about his discovery. Ross looked startled. "Your uncle, eh? Your own uncle. What was he doing here?"

"I don't know. I didn't know he was in town."

"Say, look—I hope he's not hurt bad, especially seeing as how he's your uncle—but is this *the* uncle, the one you were telling us about who has been mentioned for the Nobel Prize?"

"That's what I've been trying to tell you. He's my Uncle Donald Cargraves."

"Doctor Donald Cargraves!" Ross whistled. "Jeepers! When we start slugging people we certainly go after big game, don't we?"

"It's no laughing matter. Suppose he dies? What'll I tell my mother?"

"I wasn't laughing. Let's get over to the hospital and find out how bad he's hurt before you tell her anything. No use in worrying her unnecessarily." Ross sighed. "I guess we might as well break the news to my folks. Then I'll drive us over to the hospital."

"Didn't you tell them when you telephoned?" Morrie asked.

"No. They were out in the garden, so I just phoned and then lammed out to the curb to wait for the ambulance. They may have seen it come in the drive but I didn't wait to find out."

"I'll bet you didn't."

Ross's father was waiting for them at the house. He answered their greetings, then said, "Ross——"

"Yes, sir?"

"I heard an explosion down toward your private stamping ground. Then I saw an ambulance drive in and drive away. What happened?"

"Well, Dad, it was like this: We were making a full-power captive run on the new rocket and—" He sketched out the events.

Mr. Jenkins nodded and said, "I see. Come along, boys." He started toward the converted stable which housed the family car. "Ross, run tell your mother where we are going. Tell her I said not to worry." He went on, leaning on his cane a bit as he walked. Mr. Jenkins was a retired electrical engineer, even-tempered and taciturn.

Art could not remember his own father; Morrie's father was still living but a very different personality. Mr. Abrams ruled a large and noisy, children-cluttered household by combining a loud voice with lavish affection.

When Ross returned, puffing, his father waved away his offer to drive. "No, thank you. I want us to get there." The trip was made in silence. Mr. Jenkins left them in the foyer of the hospital with an injunction to wait.

"What do you think he will do?" Morrie asked nervously.

"I don't know. Dad'll be fair about it."

"That's what I'm afraid of," Morrie admitted. "Right now I don't want justice; I want charity."

"I hope Uncle Don is all right," Art put in.

"Huh? Oh, yes, indeed! Sorry, Art, I'm afraid we've kind of forgotten your feelings. The principal thing is for him to get well, of course."

"To tell the truth, before I knew it was Uncle Don, I was more worried over the chance that I might have gotten Mother into a law suit than I was over what we might have done to a stranger."

"Forget it," Ross advised. "A person can't help worrying over his own troubles. Dad says the test is in what you do, not in what you think. We all did what we could for him."

"Which was mostly not to touch him before the doctor came," Morrie pointed out.

"Which was what he needed."

"Yes," agreed Art, "but I don't check you, Ross, on it not mattering what you think as long as you act all right. It seems to me that wrong ideas can be just as bad as wrong ways to do things."

"Easy, now. If a guy does something brave when he's scared to death is he braver than the guy who does the same thing but isn't scared?"

16

"He's less . . . no, he's more. . . . You've got me all mixed up. It's not the same thing."

"Not quite, maybe. Skip it."

They sat in silence for a long time. Then Morrie said, "Anyhow, I hope he's all right."

Mr. Jenkins came out with news. "Well, boys, this is your lucky day. Skull uninjured according to the X-ray. The patient woke when they sewed up his scalp. I talked with him and he has decided not to scalp any of you in return." He smiled.

"May I see him?" asked Art.

"Not tonight. They've given him a hypo and he is asleep. I telephoned your mother, Art."

"You did? Thank you, sir."

"She's expecting you. I'll drop you by."

Art's interview with his mother was not too difficult; Mr. Jenkins had laid a good foundation. In fact, Mrs. Mueller was incapable of believing that Art could be "bad." But she did worry about him and Mr. Jenkins had soothed her, not only about Art but also as to the welfare of her brother.

Morrie had still less trouble with Mr. Abrams. After being assured that the innocent bystander was not badly hurt, he had shrugged. "So what? So we have lawyers in the family for such things. At fifty cents a week it'll take you about five hundred years to pay it off. Go to bed."

"Yes, Poppa."

The boys gathered at the rocket testing grounds the next morning, after being assured by a telephone call to the hospital that Doctor Cargraves had spent a good night. They planned to call on him that afternoon; at the moment they wanted to hold a post-mortem on the ill-starred *Starstruck V.*

The first job was to gather up the pieces, try to reassemble them, and then try to figure out what had happened. Art's film of the event would be necessary to complete the story, but it was not yet ready.

They were well along with the reassembling when they heard a whistle and a shout from the direction of the gate. "Hello there! Anybody home?"

"Coming!" Ross answered. They skirted the barricade to where they could see the gate. A tall, husky figure waited there—a man so young, strong, and dynamic in appearance that the bandage around his head seemed out of place, and still more so in contrast with his friendly grin.

"Uncle Don!" Art yelled as he ran up to meet him.

"Hi," said the newcomer. "You're Art. Well, you've grown a lot but you haven't changed much." He shook hands.

"What are you doing out of bed? You're sick."

"Not me," his uncle asserted. "I've got a release from the hospital to prove it. But introduce me—are these the rest of the assassins?"

"Oh—excuse me. Uncle Don, this is Maurice Abrams and this is Ross Jenkins. . . . Doctor Cargraves."

"How do you do, sir?"

"Glad to know you, Doctor."

"Glad to know you, too." Cargraves started through the gate, then hesitated. "Sure this place isn't booby-trapped?"

Ross looked worried. "Say, Doctor—we're all sorry as can be. I still can't see how it happened. The gate is covered by the barricade."

"Ricochet shot probably. Forget it. I'm not hurt. A little skin and a little blood—that's all. If I had turned back at your first warning sign, it wouldn't have happened."

"How did you happen to be coming here?"

"A fair question. I hadn't been invited, had I?"

"Oh, I didn't mean that."

"But I owe you an explanation. When I breezed into town yesterday, I already knew of the Galileo Club; Art's mother had mentioned it in letters. When my sister told me where Art was and what he was up to, I decided to slide over in hope of getting here in time to watch your test run. Your hired girl told me how to find my way out here."

"You mean you hurried out here just to see this stuff we play around with?"

"Sure. Why not? I'm interested in rockets."

"Yes, but—we really haven't got anything to show you. These are just little models."

"A new model," Doctor Cargraves answered seriously, "of anything can be important, no matter who makes it nor how small it is. I wanted to see how you work. May I?"

"Oh, certainly sir—we'd be honored."

Ross showed their guest around, with Morrie helping out and Art chipping in. Art was pink-faced and happy—this was *his* uncle, one of the world's great, a pioneer of the Atomic Age. They inspected the test stand and the control panel. Cargraves looked properly impressed and tut-tutted over the loss of *Starstruck V.*

As a matter of fact he was impressed. It is common enough in the United States for boys to build and take apart almost anything mechanical, from alarm clocks to hiked-up jaloppies. It is not so common for them to understand the sort of controlled and recorded experimentation on which science is based. Their equipment was crude and their facilities limited, but the approach was correct and the scientist recognized it.

The stainless steel mirrors used to bounce the spotlight beams over the barricade puzzled Doctor Cargraves. "Why take so much trouble to protect light bulbs?" he asked. "Bulbs are cheaper than stainless steel."

"We were able to get the mirror steel free," Ross explained. "The spotlight bulbs take cash money."

The scientist chuckled. "That reason appeals to me. Well, you fellows have certainly thrown together quite a set-up. I wish I had seen your rocket before it blew up."

"Of course the stuff we build," Ross said diffidently, "can't compare with a commerical unmanned rocket, say like a mail-carrier. But we would like to dope out something good enough to go after the junior prizes."

"Ever competed?"

"Not yet. Our physics class in high school entered one last year in the novice classification. It wasn't much—just a powder job, but that's what got us started, though we've all been crazy about rockets ever since I can remember."

"You've got some fancy control equipment. Where do you do your machine-shop work? Or do you have it done?"

"Oh, no. We do it in the high-school shop. If the shop instructor okays you, you can work after school on your own."

"It must be quite a high school," the physicist commented. "The one I went to didn't have a machine shop."

"I guess it is a pretty progressive school," Ross agreed. "It's a mechanical-arts-and-science high school and it has more courses in math and science and shop work than most. It's nice to be able to use the shops. That's where we built out telescope."

"Astronomers too, eh?"

"Well—Morrie is the astronomer of the three of us."

"Is that so?" Cargraves inquired, turning to Morrie.

Morrie shrugged. "Oh, not exactly. We all have our hobbies. Ross goes in for chemistry and rocket fuels. Art is a radio ham and a camera nut. You can study astronomy sitting down."

"I see," the physicist replied gravely. "A matter of efficient self-protection. I knew about Art's hobbies. By the way, Art, I owe you an apology; yesterday afternoon I took a look in your basement. But don't worry—I didn't touch anything."

"Oh, I'm not worried about your touching stuff, Uncle Don," Art protested, turning pinker, "but the place must have looked a mess."

"It didn't look like a drawing room but it did look like a working laboratory. I see you keep notebooks—no, I didn't touch them, either!"

"We all keep notebooks," Morrie volunteered. "That's the influence of Ross's old man."

"So?"

"Dad told me he did not care," Ross explained, "how much I messed around as long as I kept it above the tinkertoy level. He used to make me submit notes to him on everything I tried and he would grade them on clearness and completeness. After a while I got the idea and he quit."

"Does he help you with your projects?"

"Not a bit. He says they're our babies and we'll have to nurse them."

They prepared to adjourn to their clubhouse, an out-building left over from the days when the Old Ross Place was worked as a farm. They gathered up the forlorn pieces of *Starstruck V*, while Ross checked each item. "I guess that's all," he announced and started to pick up the remains.

"Wait a minute," Morrie suggested. "We never did search for the piece that clipped Doctor Cargraves."

"That's right," the scientist agreed. "I have a personal interest in that item, blunt instrument, missile, shrapnel, or whatever. I want to know how close I came to playing a harp."

Ross looked puzzled. "Come here, Art," he said in a low voice.

"I *am* here. What do you want?"

"Tell me what piece is still missing——"

"What difference does it make?" But he bent over the box containing the broken rocket and checked the items. Presently he too looked puzzled. "Ross——"

"Yeah?"

"There isn't anything missing."

"That's what *I* thought. But there has to be."

"Wouldn't it be more to the point," suggested Cargraves, "to look around near where I was hit?"

"I suppose so."

They all searched, they found nothing. Presently they organized a system which covered the ground with such thoroughness that anything larger than a medium-small ant should have come to light. They found a penny and a broken Indian arrowhead, but nothing resembling a piece of the exploded rocket.

"This is getting us nowhere," the doctor admitted. "Just where was I when you found me?"

"Right in the gateway," Morrie told him. "You were collapsed on your face and——"

"Just a minute. On my *face?*"

21

"Yes. You were——"

"But how did I get knocked on my face? I was facing toward your testing ground when the lights went out. I'm sure of that. I should have fallen backwards."

"Well . . . I'm sure you didn't, sir. Maybe it was a ricochet, as you said."

"Hmm . . . maybe." The doctor looked around. There was nothing near the gate which would make a ricochet probable. He looked at the spot where he had lain and spoke to himself.

"What did you say, Doctor?"

"Uh? Oh, nothing, nothing at all. Forget it. It was just a silly idea I had. It couldn't be." He straightened up as if dismissing the whole thing. "Let's not waste any more time on my vanishing 'blunt instrument.' It was just curiosity. Let's get on back."

The clubhouse was a one-story frame building about twenty feet square. One wall was filled with Ross's chemistry workbench with the usual clutter of test-tube racks, bunsen burners, awkward-looking, pretzel-like arrangements of glass tubing, and a double sink which looked as if it had been salvaged from a junk dealer. A home-made hood with a hinged glass front occupied one end of the bench. Parallel to the adjacent wall, in a little glass case, a precision balance of a good make but of very early vintage stood mounted on its own concrete pillar.

"We ought to have air-conditioning," Ross told the doctor, "to do really good work."

"You haven't done so badly," Cargraves commented. The boys had covered the rough walls with ply board; the cracks had been filled and the interior painted with washable enamel. The floor they had covered with linoleum, salvaged like the sink, but serviceable. The windows and door were tight. The place was clean.

"Humidity changes could play hob with some of your experiments, however," he went on. "Do you plan to put in air-conditioning sometime?"

"I doubt it. I guess the Galileo Club is about to fold up."

22

"What? Oh, that seems a shame."

"It is and it isn't. This fall we all expect to go away to Tech."

"I see. But aren't there any other members?"

"There used to be, but they've moved, gone away to school, gone in the army. I suppose we could have gotten new members but we didn't try. Well . . . we work together well and . . . you know how it is."

Cargraves nodded. He felt that he knew more explicitly than did the boy. These three were doing serious work; most of their schoolmates, even though mechanically minded, would be more interested in needling a stripped-down car up to a hundred miles an hour than in keeping careful notes. "Well, you are certainly comfortable here. It's a shame you can't take it with you."

A low, wide, padded seat stretched from wall to wall opposite the chemistry layout. The other two boys were sprawled on it, listening. Behind them, bookshelves had been built into the wall. Jules Verne crowded against Mark's *Handbook of Mechanical Engineering.* Cargraves noted other old friends: H. G. Wells' *Seven Famous Novels, The Handbook of Chemistry and Physics,* and Smyth's *Atomic Energy for Military Purposes.* Jammed in with them, side by side with Ley's *Rockets* and Eddington's *Nature of the Physical World,* were dozens of pulp magazines of the sort with robot men or space ships on their covers.

He pulled down a dog-eared copy of Haggard's *When the Earth Trembled* and settled his long body between the boys. He was beginning to feel at home. These boys he knew; he had only to gaze back through the corridors of his mind to recognize himself.

Ross said, "If you'll excuse me, I want to run up to the house."

Cargraves grunted, "Sure thing," with his nose still in the book.

Ross came back to announce, "My mother would like all of you to stay for lunch."

Morrie grinned, Art looked troubled. "My mother thinks

I eat too many meals over here as it is," he protested feebly, his eyes on his uncle.

Cargraves took him by the arm. "I'll go your bail on this one, Art," he assured him; then to Ross, "Please tell your mother that we are very happy to accept."

At lunch the adults talked, the boys listened. The scientist, his turban bandage looking stranger than ever, hit it off well with his elders. Any one would hit it off well with Mrs. Jenkins, who could have been friendly and gracious at a cannibal feast, but the boys were not used to seeing Mr. Jenkins in a chatty mood.

The boys were surprised to find out how much Mr. Jenkins knew about atomics. They had the usual low opinion of the mental processes of adults; Mr. Jenkins they respected but had subconsciously considered him the anachronism which most of his generation in fact was, a generation as a whole incapable of realizing that the world had changed completely a few years before, at Alamogordo, New Mexico, on July 16, 1945.

Yet Mr. Jenkins seemed to know who Doctor Cargraves was and seemed to know that he had been retained until recently by North American Atomics. The boys listened carefully to find out what Doctor Cargraves planned to do next, but Mr. Jenkins did not ask and Cargraves did not volunteer the information.

After lunch the three and their guest went back to the clubhouse. Cargraves spent most of the afternoon spread over the bunk, telling stories of the early days at Oak Ridge when the prospect of drowning in the inescapable, adhesive mud was more dismaying than the ever-present danger of radioactive poisoning, and the story, old but ever new and eternally exciting, of the black rainy morning in the New Mexico desert when a great purple-and-golden mushroom had climbed to the stratosphere, proclaiming that man had at last unloosed the power of the suns.

Then he shut up, claiming that he wanted to reread the

old H. Rider Haggard novel he had found. Ross and Maurice got busy at the bench; Art took a magazine. His eyes kept returning to his fabulous uncle. He noticed that the man did not seem to be turning the pages very often.

Quite a while later Doctor Cargraves put down his book. "What do you fellows know about atomics?"

The boys exchanged glances before Morrie ventured to answer. "Not much I guess. High-school physics can't touch it, really, and you can't mess with it in a home laboratory."

"That's right. But you are interested?"

"Oh, my, yes! We've read what we could—Pollard and Davidson, and Gamov's new book. But we don't have the math for atomics."

"How much math do you have?"

"Through differential equations."

"*Huh?*" Cargraves looked amazed. "Wait a minute. You guys are still in high school?"

"Just graduated."

"What kind of high school teaches differential equations? Or am I an old fuddy-duddy?"

Morrie seemed almost defensive in his explanation. "It's a new approach. You have to pass a test, then they give you algebra through quadratics, plane and spherical trigonometry, plane and solid geometry, and plane and solid analytical geometry all in one course, stirred in together. When you finish that course—and you take it as slow or as fast as you like—you go on."

Cargraves shook his head. "There've been some changes made while I was busy with the neutrons. Okay, Quiz Kids, at that rate you'll be ready for quantum theory and wave mechanics before long. But I wonder how they go about cramming you this way? Do you savvy the postulational notion in math?"

"Why, I think so."

"Tell me."

Morrie took a deep breath. "No mathematics has any reality of its own, not even common arithmetic. All mathematics is purely an invention of the mind, with no connection with the world around us, except that we find some mathematics convenient in describing things."

"Go on. You're doing fine!"

"Even then it isn't real—or isn't 'true'—the way the ancients thought of it. Any system of mathematics is derived from purely arbitrary assumptions, called 'postulates,' the sort of thing the ancients called 'axioms.' "

"Your jets are driving, kid! How about the operational notion in scientific theory? No . . . Art—you tell me."

Art looked embarrassed; Morrie looked pleased but relieved. "Well, uh . . . the operational idea is, uh, it's building up your theory in terms of the operations you perform, like measuring, or timing, so that you don't go reading into the experiments things that aren't there."

Cargraves nodded. "That's good enough—it shows you know what you're talking about." He kept quiet for a long time, then he added, "You fellows really interested in rockets?"

Ross answered this time, "Why, er, yes, we are. Rockets among other things. We would certainly like to have a go at those junior prizes."

"That's all?"

"Well, no, not exactly. I guess we all think, well, maybe some day . . ." His voice trailed off.

"I think I see." Cargraves sat up. "But why bother with the competition? After all, as you pointed out, model rockets can't touch the full-sized commercial jobs. The prizes are offered just to keep up interest in rocketry—it's like the model airplane meets they used to have when I was a kid. But you guys can do better than that—why don't you go in for the *senior prizes?*"

Three sets of eyes were fixed on him. "What do you mean?"

Cargraves shrugged. "Why don't you go to the moon—with me?"

III   CUT-RATE COLUMBUS

THE SILENCE THAT FILLED THE clubhouse had a solid quality, as if one could slice it and make sandwiches. Ross recovered his voice first. "You don't mean it," he said in a hushed tone.

"But I do," Doctor Cargraves answered evenly. "I mean it quite seriously. I propose to try to make a trip to the moon. I'd like to have you fellows with me. Art," he added, "close your mouth. You'll make a draft."

Art gulped, did as he was told, then promptly opened it again. "But look," he said, his words racing, "Uncle Don . . . if you take us—I mean, how could we—or if we did, what would we use for—how do you propose——"

"Easy, easy!" Cargraves protested. "All of you keep quiet and I'll tell you what I have in mind. Then you can think it over and tell me whether or not you want to go for it."

Morrie slapped the bench beside him. "I don't care," he said, "I don't care if you're going to try to fly there on your worn broom—I'm in. I'm going along."

"So am I," Ross added quickly, moistening his lips.

Art looked wildly at the other two. "But I didn't mean that I wasn't—I was just asking— Oh, shucks! Me, too! You know that."

The young scientist gave the impression of bowing without getting up. "Gentlemen, I appreciate the confidence you place in me. But you are not committed to anything just yet."

27

"But——"

"So kindly pipe down," he went on, "and I'll lay out my cards, face up. Then we'll talk. Have you guys ever taken an oath?"

"Oh, sure—Scout Oath, anyhow."

"I was a witness in court once."

"Fine. I want you all to promise, on your honor, not to spill anything I tell you without my specific permission, whether we do business or not. It is understood that you are not bound thereby to remain silent if you are morally obligated to speak up—you are free to tell on me if there are moral or legal reasons why you should. Otherwise, you keep mum—on your honor. How about it?"

"Yes, sir!" "Right!" "Check."

"Okay," agreed Cargraves, settling back on his spine. "That was mostly a matter of form, to impress you with the necessity of keeping your lips buttoned. You'll understand why, later. Now here is the idea: All my life I've wanted to see the day when men would conquer space and explore the planets—and I wanted to take part in it. I don't have to tell you how that feels." He waved a hand at the book shelves. "Those books show me you understand it; you've got the madness yourselves. Besides that, what I saw out on your rocket grounds, what I see here, what I saw yesterday when I sneaked a look in Art's lab, shows me that you aren't satisfied just to dream about it and read about it—you want to *do* something. Right?"

"Right!" It was a chorus.

Cargraves nodded. "I felt the same way. I took my first degree in mechanical engineering with the notion that rockets were mechanical engineering and that I would need the training. I worked as an engineer after graduation until I had saved up enough to go back to school. I took my doctor's degree in atomic physics, because I had a hunch—oh, I wasn't the only one!—I had a hunch that atomic power was needed for practical space ships. Then came the war and the Manhattan Project.

"When the Atomic Age opened up a lot of people pre-

28

dicted that space flight was just around the corner. But it didn't work out that way—nobody knew how to harness the atom to a rocket. Do you know why?"

Somewhat hesitantly Ross spoke up. "Yes, I think I do."

"Go ahead."

"Well, for a rocket you need mass times velocity, quite a bit of mass in what the jet throws out and plenty of velocity. But in an atomic reaction there isn't very much mass and the energy comes out in radiations in all directions instead of a nice, lined-up jet. Just the same——"

" 'Just the same' what?"

"Well, there *ought* to be a way to harness all that power. Darn it—with so much power from so little weight, there ought to be *some* way."

"Just what I've always thought," Cargraves said with a grin. "We've built atomic plants that turn out more power than Boulder Dam. We've made atomic bombs that make the two used in the war seem like firecrackers. Power to burn, power to throw away. Yet we haven't been able to hook it to a rocket. Of course there are other problems. An atomic power plant takes a lot of shielding to protect the operators—you know that. And that means weight. Weight is everything in a rocket. If you add another hundred pounds in dead load, you have to pay for it in fuel. Suppose your shield weighed only a ton—how much fuel would that cost you, Ross?"

Ross scratched his head. "I don't know what kind of fuel you mean nor what kind of a rocket you are talking about —what you want it to do."

"Fair enough," the scientist admitted. "I asked you an impossible question. Suppose we make it a chemical fuel and a moon rocket and assume a mass-ratio of twenty to one. Then for a shield weighing a ton we have to carry twenty tons of fuel."

Art sat up suddenly. "Wait a minute, Uncle Don."

"Yes?"

"If you use a *chemical* fuel, like alcohol and liquid oxygen say, then you won't need a radiation shield."

29

"You got me, kid. But that was just for illustration. If you had a decent way to use atomic power, you might be able to hold your mass-ratio down to, let's say, one-to-one. Then a one-ton shield would only require one ton of fuel to carry it. That suit you better?"

Art wriggled in excitement. "I'll say it does. That means a *real* space ship. We could go anywhere in it!"

"But we're still on earth," his uncle pointed out dryly. "I said '*if*.' Don't burn out your jets before you take off. And there is still a third hurdle: atomic power plants are fussy to control—hard to turn on, hard to turn off. But we can let that one alone till we come to it. I still think we'll get to the moon."

He paused. They waited expectantly.

"I think I've got a way to apply atomic power to rockets." Nobody stood up. Nobody cheered. No one made a speech starting, "On this historic occasion—" Instead they held their breaths, waiting for him to go on.

"Oh, I'm not going into details now. You'll find out all about it, if we work together."

"We will!" "Sure thing!"

"I hope so. I tried to interest the company I was with in the scheme, but they wouldn't hold still."

"Gee whillickers! Why not?"

"Corporations are in business to make money; they owe that to their stockholders. Do you see any obvious way to make money out of a flight to the moon?"

"Shucks." Art tossed it off. "They ought to be willing to risk going broke to back a thing like this."

"Nope. You're off the beam, kid. Remember they are handling other people's money. Have you any idea how much it would cost to do the research and engineering development, using the ordinary commercial methods, for anything as big as a trip to the moon?"

"No," Art admitted. "A good many thousands, I suppose." Morrie spoke up. "More like a hundred thousand."

"That's closer. The technical director of our company made up a tentative budget of a million and a quarter."

"Whew!"

"Oh, he was just showing that it was not commercially practical. He wanted to adapt my idea to power plants for ships and trains. So I handed in my resignation."

"Good for you!"

Morrie looked thoughtful. "I guess I see," he said slowly, "why you swore us to secrecy. They own your idea."

Cargraves shook his head emphatically, "No, not at all. You certainly would be entitled to squawk if I tried to get you into a scheme to jump somebody else's patent rights—even if they held them by a yellow-dog, brain-picking contract." Cargraves spoke with vehemence. "My contract wasn't that sort. The company owns the idea for the purposes for which the research was carried out—power. And I own anything else I see in it. We parted on good terms. I don't blame them. When the queen staked Columbus, nobody dreamed that he would come back with the Empire State Building in his pocket."

"Hey," said Ross, "these senior prizes—they aren't big enough. That's why nobody has made a real bid for the top ones. The prize wouldn't pay the expenses, not for the kind of budget you mentioned. It's a sort of a swindle, isn't it?"

"Not a swindle, but that's about the size of it," Cargraves conceded. "With the top prize only $250,000 it won't tempt General Electric, or du Pont, or North American Atomic, or any other big research corporation. They can't afford it, unless some other profit can be seen. As a matter of fact, a lot of the prize money comes from those corporations." He sat up again. "But we can compete for it!"

"How?"

"I don't give a darn about the prize money. I just want to go!" "Me too!" Ross made the statement; Art chimed in.

"My sentiments exactly. As to how, that's where you come in. I can't spend a million dollars, but I think there is a way to tackle this on a shoestring. We need a ship. We need the fuel. We need a lot of engineering and mechanical work.

31

We need overhead expenses and supplies for the trip. I've got a ship."

"You have? Now? A *space ship?*" Art was wide-eyed.

"I've got an option to buy an Atlantic freighter-rocket at scrap prices. I can swing that. It's a good rocket, but they are replacing the manned freighters with the more economical robot-controlled jobs. It's a V-17 and it isn't fit to convert to passenger service, so we get it as scrap. But if I buy it, it leaves me almost broke. Under the UN trusteeship for atomics, a senior member of the Global Association of Atomic Scientists—that's me!" he stuck in, grinning, "can get fissionable material for experimental purposes, if the directors of the Association approve. I can swing that. I've picked thorium, rather than uranium-235, or plutonium— never mind why. But the project itself had me stumped, just too expensive. I was about ready to try to promote it by endorsements and lecture contracts and all the other claptrap it sometimes takes to put over scientific work—when I met you fellows."

He got up and faced them. "I don't need much to convert that old V-17 into a space ship. But I do need skilled hands and brains and the imagination to know what is needed and why. You'd be my mechanics and junior engineers and machine-shop workers and instrument men and presently my crew. You'll do hard, dirty work for long hours and cook your own meals in the bargain. You'll get nothing but coffee-and-cakes and a chance to break your necks. The ship may never leave the ground. If it does, chances are you'll never live to tell about it. It won't be one big adventure. I'll work you till you're sick of me and probably nothing will come of it. But that's the proposition. Think it over and let me know."

There was the nerve-tingling pause which precedes an earthquake. Then the boys were on their feet, shouting all at once. It was difficult to make out words, but the motion had been passed by acclamation; the Galileo Club intended to go to the moon.

When the buzzing had died down, Cargraves noticed that

Ross's face was suddenly grave. "What's the matter, Ross? Cold feet already?"

"No," Ross shook his head. "I'm afraid it's too good to be true."

"Could be, could be. I think I know what's worrying you. Your parents?"

"Uh, huh. I doubt if our folks will ever let us do it."

IV THE BLOOD OF PIONEERS

CARGRAVES LOOKED AT THEIR woebegone faces. He knew what they were faced with; a boy can't just step up to his father and say, "By the way, old man, count me out on those plans we made for me to go to college. I've got a date to meet Santa Claus at the North Pole." It was the real reason he had hesitated before speaking of his plans. Finally he said, "I'm afraid it's up to each of you. Your promise to me does not apply to your parents, but ask them to respect your confidence. I don't want our plans to get into the news."

"But look, Doctor Cargraves," Morrie put in, "why be so secret about it? It might make our folks feel that it was just a wild-eyed kid's dream. Why can't you just go to them and explain where we would fit into it?"

"No," Cargraves answered, "they are *your* parents. When and if they want to see me, I'll go to them and try to give satisfactory answers. But you will have to convince them that you mean business. As to secrecy, the reasons are these: there is only one aspect of my idea that can be patented and, under the rules of the UN Atomics Convention, it can be licensed by any one who wants to use it. The company is obtaining the patent, but not as a rocket device. The idea that I can apply it to a cheap, shoestring venture into space travel is mine and I don't want any one else to beat me to it with more money and stronger backing. Just before we are ready to leave we will call in the reporters—probably to run a story about how we busted our necks on the take-off.

"But I see your point," he went on. "We don't want this to look like a mad-scientist-and-secret-laboratory set-up. Well, I'll try to convince them."

Doctor Cargraves made an exception in the case of Art's mother, because she was his own sister. He cautioned Art to retire to his basement laboratory as soon as dinner was over and then, after helping with the dishes, spoke to her. She listened quietly while he explained. "Well, what do you think of it?"

She sat very still, her eyes everywhere but on his face, her hands busy twisting and untwisting her handkerchief. "Don, you can't do this to me."

He waited for her to go on.

"I can't let him go, Don. He's all I've got. With Hans gone. . . ."

"I know that," the doctor answered gently. "But Hans has been gone since Art was a baby. You can't limit the boy on that account."

"Do you think that makes it any easier?" She was close to tears.

"No, I don't. But it is on Hans' account that you must not keep his son in cotton batting. Hans had courage to burn. If he had been willing to knuckle under to the Nazis he would have stayed at Kaiser Wilhelm Institute. But Hans was a scientist. He wouldn't trim his notion of truth to fit political gangsters. He——"

"And it killed him!"

"I know, I know. But remember, Grace, it was only the fact that you were an American girl that enabled you to pull enough strings to get him out of the concentration camp."

"I don't see what that's got to do with it. Oh, you should have seen him when they let him out!" She was crying now.

"I did see him when you brought him to this country," he said gently, "and that was bad enough. But the fact that you are American has a lot to do with it. We have a tradition of freedom, personal freedom, scientific freedom. That freedom isn't kept alive by caution and unwillingness to take risks. If Hans were alive he would be going with me—you know that, Sis. You owe it to his son not to keep him caged. You can't keep him tied to your apron strings forever, anyhow. A few more years and you will have to let him follow his own bent."

Her head was bowed. She did not answer. He patted her shoulder. "You think it over, Sis. I'll try to bring him back in one piece."

When Art came upstairs, much later, his mother was still sitting, waiting for him. "Arthur?"

"Yes, Mother."

"You want to go to the moon?"

"Yes, Mother."

She took a deep breath, then replied steadily. "You be a good boy on the moon, Arthur. You do what your uncle tells you to."

"I will, Mother."

Morrie managed to separate his father from the rest of the swarming brood shortly after dinner. "Poppa, I want to talk to you man to man."

"And how else?"

"Well, this is different. I know you wanted me to come into the business, but you agreed to help me go to Tech."

His father nodded. "The business will get along. Scientists we are proud to have in the family. Your Uncle Bernard is a fine surgeon. Do we ask him to help with the business?"

"Yes, Poppa, but that's just it—I don't want to go to Tech."

"So? Another school?"

"No, I don't want to go to school." He explained Doctor Cargraves' scheme, blurting it out as fast as possible in an attempt to give his father the whole picture before he set his mind. Finished, he waited.

His father rocked back and forth. "So it's the moon now, is it? And maybe next week the sun. A man should settle down if he expects to accomplish anything, Maurice."

"But, Poppa, *this* is what I want to accomplish!"

"When do you expect to start?"

"You mean you'll let me? I *can?*"

"Not so fast, Maurice. I did not say yes; I did not say no. It has been quite a while since you stood up before the congregation and made your speech, 'Today I am a man—' That meant you were a man, Maurice, right that moment. It's not for me to let you; it's for me to advise you. I advise you not to. I think it's foolishness."

Morrie stood silent, stubborn but respectful.

"Wait a week, then come back and tell me what you are going to do. There's a pretty good chance that you will break your neck on this scheme, isn't there?"

"Well . . . yes, I suppose so."

"A week isn't too long to make up your mind to kill yourself. In the meantime, don't talk to Momma about this."

"Oh, I won't!"

"If you decide to go ahead anyway, I'll break the news to her. Momma isn't going to like this, Maurice."

Doctor Donald Cargraves received a telephone call the next morning which requested him, if convenient, to come to the Jenkins' home. He did so, feeling, unreasonably he thought, as if he were being called in on the carpet. He found Mr. and Mrs. Jenkins in the drawing room; Ross was not in sight.

Mr. Jenkins shook hands with him and offered him a chair. "Cigarette, Doctor? Cigar?"

"Neither, thank you."

"If you smoke a pipe," Mrs. Jenkins added, "please do so."

Cargraves thanked her and gratefully stoked up his old stinker.

"Ross tells me a strange story," Mr. Jenkins started in. "If he were not pretty reliable I'd think his imagination was working overtime. Perhaps you can explain it."

"I'll try, sir."

"Thanks. Is it true, Doctor, that you intend to try to make a trip to the moon?"

"Quite true."

"Well! Is it also true that you have invited Ross and his chums to go with you in this fantastic adventure?"

"Yes, it is." Doctor Cargraves found that he was biting hard on the stem of his pipe.

Mr. Jenkins stared at him. "I'm amazed. Even if it were something safe and sane, your choice of boys as partners strikes me as outlandish."

Cargraves explained why he believed the boys could be competent junior partners in the enterprise. "In any case," he concluded, "being young is not necessarily a handicap. The great majority of the scientists in the Manhattan Project were very young men."

"But not boys, Doctor."

"Perhaps not. Still, Sir Isaac Newton was a boy when he invented the calculus. Professor Einstein himself was only twenty-six when he published his first paper on relativity—and the work had been done when he was still younger. In mechanics and in the physical sciences, calendar age has nothing to do with the case; it's solely a matter of training and ability."

"Even if what you say is true, Doctor, training takes time and these boys have not had time for the training you need for such a job. It takes years to make an engineer, still more years to make a toolmaker or an instrument man. Tarnation, I'm an engineer myself. I know what I'm talking about."

"Ordinarily I would agree with you. But these boys have what I need. Have you looked at their work?"

"Some of it."

"How good is it?"

"It's good work—within the limits of what they know."

"But what they know is just what I need for this job. They are rocket fans now. They've learned in their hobbies the specialties I need."

Mr. Jenkins considered this, then shook his head. "I suppose there is something in what you say. But the scheme is fantastic. I don't say that space flight is fantastic; I expect that the engineering problems involved will some day be solved. But space flight is not a back-yard enterprise. When it comes it will be done by the air forces, or as a project of one of the big corporations, not by half-grown boys."

Cargraves shook his head. "The government won't do it. It would be laughed off the floor of Congress. As for corporations, I have reason to be almost certain they won't do it, either."

Mr. Jenkins looked at him quizzically. "Then it seems to me that we're not likely to see space flight in our lifetimes."

"I wouldn't say so," the scientist countered. "The United States isn't the only country on the globe. It wouldn't surprise me to hear some morning that the Russians had done it. They've got the technical ability and they seem to be willing to spend money on science. They might do it."

"Well, what if they do?"

Cargraves took a deep breath. "I have nothing against the Russians; if they beat me to the moon, I'll take off my hat to them. But I prefer our system to theirs; it would be a sour day for us if it turned out that they could do something as big and as wonderful as this when we weren't even prepared to tackle it, under our set-up. Anyhow," he continued, "I have enough pride in my own land to want it to be *us*, rather than some other country."

Mr. Jenkins nodded and changed his tack. "Even if these three boys have the special skills you need, I still don't see why you picked boys. Frankly, that's why the scheme looks rattlebrained to me. You should have experienced engineers and mechanics and your crew should be qualified rocket pilots."

Doctor Cargraves laid the whole thing before them, and

explained how he hoped to carry out his plans on a slim budget. When he had finished Mr. Jenkins said, "Then as a matter of fact you braced these three boys because you were hard up for cash?"

"If you care to put it that way."

"I didn't put it that way; you did. Candidly, I don't altogether approve of your actions. I don't think you meant any harm, but you didn't stop to think. I don't thank you for getting Ross and his friends stirred up over a matter unsuited to their ages without consulting their parents first."

Donald Cargraves felt his mouth grow tense but said nothing; he felt that he could not explain that he had lain awake much of the night over misgivings of just that sort.

"However," Mr. Jenkins went on, "I understand your disappointment and sympathize with your enthusiasm." He smiled briefly. "I'll make you a deal. I'll hire three mechanics —you pick them—and one junior engineer or physicist, to help you in converting your ship. When the time comes, I'll arrange for a crew. Hiring will not be needed there, in my opinion—we will be able to pick from a long list of volunteers. Wait a minute," he said, as Cargraves started to speak, "you'll be under no obligation to me. We will make it a business proposition of a speculative sort. We'll draw up a contract under which, if you make it, you assign to me a proper percentage of the prize money and of the profits from exclusive news stories, books, lectures, and so forth. Does that look like a way out?"

Cargraves took a deep breath. "Mr. Jenkins," he said slowly, "if I had had that proposition last week, I would have jumped at it. But I can't take it."

"Why not?"

"I can't let the boys down. I'm already committed."

"Would it make a difference if I told you there was absolutely no chance of Ross being allowed to go?"

"No. I will have to go looking for just such a backer as yourself, but it can't be you. It would smack too much of allowing myself to be bought off— No offense intended, Mr. Jenkins!—to welch on the proposition I made Ross."

Mr. Jenkins nodded. "I was afraid you would feel that way. I respect your attitude, Doctor. Let me call Ross in and tell him the outcome." He started for the door.

"Just a moment, Mr. Jenkins——"

"Yes?"

"I want to tell you that I respect your attitude, too. As I told you, the project is dangerous, quite dangerous. I think it is a proper danger but I don't deny your right to forbid your son to risk his neck with me."

"I am afraid you don't understand me, Doctor Cargraves. It's dangerous, certainly, and naturally that worries me and Mrs. Jenkins, but that is not my objection. I would not try to keep Ross out of danger. I let him take flying lessons; I even had something to do with getting two surplus army trainers for the high school. I haven't tried to keep him from playing around with explosives. That's not the reason."

"May I ask what it is?"

"Of course. Ross is scheduled to start in at the Technical Institute this fall. I think it's more important for him to get a sound basic education than for him to be first man on the moon." He turned away again.

"Wait a minute! If it's his education you are worried about, would you consider me a competent teacher?"

"Eh? Well . . . yes."

"I will undertake to tutor the boys in technical and engineering subjects. I will see to it that they do not fall behind."

Mr. Jenkins hesitated momentarily. "No, Doctor, the matter is settled. An engineer without a degree has two strikes against him to start with. Ross is going to get his degree." He stepped quickly to the door and called out, "Ross!"

"Coming, Dad." The center of the argument ran downstairs and into the room. He looked around, first at Cargraves, then anxiously at his father, and finally at his mother, who looked up from her knitting and smiled at him but did not speak. "What's the verdict?" he inquired.

His father put it bluntly. "Ross, you start in school in the fall. I cannot okay this scheme."

Ross's jaw muscles twitched but he did not answer directly. Instead he said to Cargraves, "How about Art and Morrie?"

"Art's going. Morrie phoned me and said his father didn't think much of it but would not forbid it."

"Does that make any difference, Dad?"

"I'm afraid not. I don't like to oppose you, son, but when it comes right down to cases, I am responsible for you until you are twenty-one. You've got to get your degree."

"But . . . but . . . look, Dad. A degree isn't everything. If the trip is successful, I'll be so famous that I won't need a tag on my name to get a job. And if I don't come back, I won't need a degree!"

Mr. Jenkins shook his head. "Ross, my mind is made up."

Cargraves could see that Ross was fighting to keep the tears back. Somehow it made him seem older, not younger. When he spoke again his voice was unsteady. "Dad?"

"Yes, Ross?"

"If I can't go, may I at least go along to help with the rebuilding job? They'll need help."

Cargraves looked at him with new interest. He had some comprehension of what the proposal would cost the boy in heartache and frustration.

Mr. Jenkins looked surprised but answered quickly. "You may do that—up till the time school opens."

"Suppose they aren't through by then? I wouldn't want to walk out on them."

"Very well. If necessary you can start school the second semester. That is my last concession." He turned to Doctor Cargraves. "I shall count on you for some tutoring." Then to his son, "But that is the end of the matter, Ross. When you are twenty-one you can risk your neck in a space ship if you like. Frankly, I expect that there will still be plenty of chance for you to attempt the first flight to the moon if you are determined to try it." He stood up.

"Albert."

"Eh? Yes, Martha?" He turned deferentially to his wife. She laid her knitting in her lap and spoke emphatically. "Let him go, Albert!"

"Eh? What do you mean, my dear?"

"I mean, let the boy go to the moon, if he can.

"I know what I said, and you've put up a good argument for me. But I've listened and learned. Doctor Cargraves is right; I was wrong. We can't expect to keep them in the nest.

"Oh, I know what I said," she went on, "but a mother is bound to cry a little. Just the same, this country was not built by people who were afraid to go. Ross's great-great-grandfather crossed the mountains in a Conestoga wagon and homesteaded this place. He was nineteen, his bride was seventeen. It's a matter of family record that their parents opposed the move." She stirred suddenly and one of her knitting needles broke. "I would hate to think that I had let the blood run thin." She got up and went quickly from the room.

Mr. Jenkins' shoulders sagged. "You have my permission, Ross," he said presently. "Doctor, I wish you good luck. And now, if you will excuse me . . ." He followed his wife.

V GROWING PAINS

"How much farther?" The noise of the stripped-down car combined with desert wind caused Art to shout.

"Look at the map," Ross said, his hands busy at the wheel in trying to avoid a jack rabbit. "It's fifty-three miles from

Route 66 to the turn-off, then seven miles on the turn-off."

"We left Highway 66 about thirty-nine, forty miles back," Art replied. "We ought to be in sight of the turn-off before long." He squinted out across bare, colorful New Mexico countryside. "Did you ever see so much wide-open, useless country? Cactus and coyotes—what's it good for?"

"I like it," Ross answered. "Hang on to your hat." There was a flat, straight stretch ahead, miles along; Ross peeled off and made the little car dig . . . seventy . . . eighty . . . ninety . . . ninety-five. The needle quivered up toward three figures.

"Hey, Ross?"

"Yeah?"

"This rig ain't young any more. Why crack us up?"

"Sissy," said Ross, but he eased up on the gas.

"Not at all," Art protested. "If we kill ourselves trying to get to the moon, fine—we're heroes. But if we bust our fool necks before we start, we'll just look silly."

"Okay, okay—is that the turn-off?"

A dirt road swung off to the right and took out over the desert. They followed it about a quarter of a mile, then pulled up at a steel gate barring the road. A strong fence, topped by barbed wire, stretched out in both directions. There was a sign on the gate:

DANGER

Unexploded Shells

Enter this area at your own risk.
Disturb nothing—report all suspi-
cious objects to the District Forester.

"This is it," Ross stated. "Got the keys?" The area beyond was an abandoned training ground of the war, part of more than 8,000,000 acres in the United States which had been rendered useless until decontaminated by the hazardous efforts of army engineer specialists. This desert area was not worth the expense and risk of decontamination, but it was ideal for Cargraves; it assured plenty of room and no innocent bystanders—and it was rent free, loaned to the Association of Atomic Scientists, on Cargraves' behalf.

Art chucked Ross some keys. Ross tried them, then said, "You've given me the wrong keys."

"I don't think so. Nope," he continued, "those are the keys Doc sent."

"What do we do?"

"Bust the lock, maybe."

"Not this lock. Do we climb it?"

"With the rig under one arm? Be your age."

A car crawled toward them, its speed lost in the vastness of the desert. It stopped near them and a man in a military Stetson stuck his head out. "Hey, there!"

Art muttered, "Hey, yourself," then said, "Good morning."

"What are you trying to do?"

"Get inside."

"Don't you see the sign? Wait a minute—either one of you named Jenkins?"

"He's Ross Jenkins. I'm Art Mueller."

"Pleased to know you. I'm the ranger hereabouts. Name o' Buchanan. I'll let you in, but I don't rightly know as I should."

"Why not?" Ross's tone was edgy. He felt that they were being sized up as youngsters.

"Well . . . we had a little accident in there the other day. That's why the lock was changed."

"Accident?"

"Man got in somehow—no break in the fence. He tangled with a land mine about a quarter of a mile this side of your cabin."

"Did it . . . kill him?"

"Deader 'n a door nail. I spotted it by the buzzards. See here—I'll let you in; I've got a copy of your permit. But don't go exploring. You stay in the marked area around the cabin, and stay on the road that follows the power line."

Ross nodded. "We'll be careful."

"Mind you are. What are you young fellows going to do in there, anyway? Raise jack rabbits?"

"That's right. Giant jack rabbits, eight feet tall."

"So? Well, keep 'em inside the marked area, or you'll have jack rabbit hamburger."

"We'll be careful," Ross repeated. "Any idea who the man was that had the accident? Or what he was doing here?"

"None, on both counts. The buzzards didn't leave enough to identify. Doesn't make sense. There was nothing to steal in there; it was before your stuff came."

"Oh, it's here!"

"Yep. You'll find the crates stacked out in the open. He wasn't a desert man," the Ranger went on. "You could tell by his shoes. Must 'a' come by car, but there was no car around. Doesn't make sense."

"No, it doesn't seem to," Ross agreed, "but he's dead, so that ends it."

"Correct. Here are your keys. Oh, yes—" He put his hand back in his pocket. "Almost forgot. Telegram for you."

"For us? Oh, thanks!"

"Better put up a mail box out at the highway," Buchanan suggested. "This reached you by happenstance."

"We'll do that," Ross agreed absently, as he tore open the envelope.

"So long." Buchanan kicked his motor into life.

"So long, and thanks again."

"For Heaven's sake, what does it say?" Art demanded.

"Read it:"

PASSED FINAL TESTS TODAY. LEAVING SATUR-DAY. PLEASE PROVIDE BRASS BAND, DANCING GIRLS, AND TWO FATTED CALVES—ONE RARE, ONE MEDIUM. (signed) DOC AND MORRIE.

Ross grinned. "Imagine that! Old Morrie a rocket pilot! I'll bet his hat doesn't fit him now."

"I'll bet it doesn't. Darn! We all should have taken the course."

"Relax, relax. Don't be small about it—we'd have wasted half the summer." Ross dismissed the matter.

Art himself did not understand his own jealousy. Deep inside, it was jealousy of the fact that Morrie had been able to go to Spaatz Field in the company of Art's idolized uncle rather than the purpose of the trip. All the boys had had dual-control airplane instruction; Morrie had gone on and gotten a private license. Under the rules—out of date, in Art's opinion—an airplane pilot could take a shortened course for rocket pilot. Doctor Cargraves held a slightly dusty aircraft license some fifteen years old. He had been planning to qualify for rocket operation; when he found that Morrie was eligible it was natural to include him.

This had left Ross and Art to carry out numerous chores for the enterprise, then to make their own way to New Mexico to open up the camp.

The warning to follow the power line had been necessary; the boys found the desert inside pock-marked by high explosive and criss-crossed with tracks, one as good as another, carved years before by truck and tank and mobile carrier. The cabin itself they found to be inside a one-strand corral a quarter of a mile wide and over a mile long. Several hundred yards beyond the corral and stretching away for miles toward the horizon was an expanse which looked like a green, rippling lake—the glassy crater of the atom bomb test of 1951, the UN's Doomsday Bomb.

Neither the cabin nor the piled-up freight could hold their attention until they had looked at it. Ross drove the car to the far side of the enclosure and they stared.

Art gave a low respectful whistle. "How would you like to have been under that?" Ross inquired in a hushed voice.

"Not any place in the same county—or the next county. How would you like to be in a city when one of those things goes off?"

Ross shook his head. "I want to zig when it zags. Art, they better never have to drop another one, except in practice. If they ever start lobbing those things around, it 'ud be the end of civilization."

"They won't," Art assured him. "What d'you think the UN police is for? Wars are out. Everybody knows that."

"You know it and I know it. But I wonder if everybody knows it?"

"It'll be just too bad if they don't."

"Yeah—too bad for *us*."

Art climbed out of the car. "I wonder if we can get down to it?"

"Well, don't try. We'll find out later."

"There can't be any duds in the crater or anywhere in the area—not after that."

"Don't forget our friend that the buzzards ate. Duds that weren't exposed to the direct blast might not go off. This bomb was set off about five miles up."

"Huh? I thought——"

"You were thinking about the test down in Chihuahua. That was a ground job. Come on. We got work to do." He trod on the starter.

The cabin was pre-fab, moved in after the atom bomb test to house the radioactivity observers. It had not been used since and looked it. "Whew! What a mess," Art remarked. "We should have brought a tent."

"It'll be all right when we get it fixed up. Did you see kerosene in that stuff outside?"

"Two drums of it."

"Okay. I'll see if I can make this stove work. I could use some lunch." The cabin was suitable, although dirty. It had a drilled well; the water was good, although it had a strange taste. There were six rough bunks needing only bedding rolls. The kitchen was the end of the room, the dining room a large pine table, but there were shelves, hooks on the walls, windows, a tight roof overhead. The stove worked well, even though it was smelly; Ross produced scrambled eggs, coffee, bread and butter, German-fried potatoes, and a bakery apple pie with only minor burns and mishaps.

It took all day to clean the cabin, unload the car, and uncrate what they needed at once. By the time they finished supper, prepared this time by Art, they were glad to crawl into their sacks. Ross was snoring gently before Art closed his eyes. Between Ross's snores and the mournful howls of distant coyotes Art was considering putting plugs in his ears, when the morning sun woke him up.

"Get up, Ross!"

"Huh? What? Wassamatter?"

"Show a leg. We're burning daylight."

"I'm tired," Ross answered as he snuggled back into the bedding. "I think I'll have breakfast in bed."

"You and your six brothers. Up you come—today we pour the foundation for the shop."

"That's right." Ross crawled regretfully out of bed. "Wonderful weather—I think I'll take a sun bath."

"I think you'll get breakfast, while I mark out the job."

"Okay, Simon Legree."

The machine shop was a sheet metal and stringer affair, to be assembled. They mixed the cement with the sandy soil of the desert, which gave them a concrete good enough for a temporary building. It was necessary to uncrate the power tools and measure them before the fastening bolts could be imbedded in the concrete. Ross watched as Art placed the last bolt. "You sure we got 'em all?"

"Sure. Grinder, mill, lathe—" He ticked them off. "Drill press, both saws—" They had the basic tools needed for almost any work. Then they placed bolts for the structure itself, matching the holes in the metal sills to the bolts as they set them in the wet concrete. By nightfall they had sections of the building laid out, each opposite its place, ready for assembly.

"Do you think the power line will carry the load?" Art said anxiously, as they knocked off.

Ross shrugged. "We won't be running all the tools at once. Quit worrying, or we'll never get to the moon. We've got to wash dishes before we can get supper."

By Saturday the tools had been hooked up and tested,

and Art had rewound one of the motors. The small mountain of gear had been stowed and the cabin was clean and reasonably orderly. They discovered in unpacking cases that several had been broken open, but nothing seemed to have been hurt. Ross was inclined to dismiss the matter, but Art was worried. His precious radio and electronic equipment had been gotten at.

"Quit fretting," Ross advised him. "Tell Doc about it when he comes. The stuff was insured."

"It was insured *in transit*," Art pointed out. "By the way, when do you think they will get here?"

"I can't say," Ross answered. "If they come by train, it might be Tuesday or later. If they fly to Albuquerque and take the bus, it might be tomorrow—what was that?" He glanced up.

"Where?" asked Art.

"There. Over there, to your left. Rocket."

"So it is! It must be a military job; we're off the commercial routes. Hey, he's turned on his nose jets!"

"He's going to land. He's going to land *here!*"

"You don't suppose?"

"I don't know. I thought—there he comes! It can't—" His words were smothered when the thunderous, express-train roar reached them, as the rocket decelerated. Before the braking jets had been applied, it was traveling ahead of its own din, and had been, for them, as silent as thought. The pilot put it down smoothly not more than five hundred yards from them, with a last blast of the nose and belly jets which killed it neatly.

They began to run.

As they panted up to the sleek, gray sides of the craft, the door forward of the stub wings opened and a tall figure jumped down, followed at once by a smaller man.

"Doc! Doc! Morrie!"

"Hi, sports!" Cargraves yelled. "Well, we made it. Is lunch ready?"

Morrie was holding himself straight, almost popping with repressed emotion. "*I* made the landing," he announced.

"You did?" Art seemed incredulous.

"Sure. Why not? I got my license. Want to see it?"

" 'Hot Pilot Abrams,' it says here," Ross alleged, as they examined the document. "But why didn't you put some glide on it? You practically set her down on her jets."

"Oh, I was practicing for the moon landing."

"You were, huh? Well, Doc makes the moon landing or I guarantee I don't go."

Cargraves interrupted the kidding. "Take it easy. Neither one of us will try an airless landing."

Morrie looked startled. Ross said, "Then who——"

"Art will make the moon landing."

Art gulped and said, "Who? Me?"

"In a way. It will have to be a radar landing; we can't risk a crack-up on anything as hard as an all-jet landing when there is no way to walk home. Art will have to modify the circuits to let the robot-pilot do it. But Morrie will be the stand-by," he went on, seeing the look on Morrie's face. "Morrie's reaction time is better than mine. I'm getting old. Now how about lunch? I want to change clothes and get to work."

Morrie was dressed in a pilot's coverall, but Cargraves was wearing his best business suit. Art looked him over. "How come the zoot suit, Uncle? You don't look like you expected to come by rocket. For that matter, I thought the ship was going to be ferried out?"

"Change in plans. I came straight from Washington to the field and Morrie took off as soon as I arrived. The ship was ready, so we brought it out ourselves, and saved about five hundred bucks in ferry pilot charges."

"Everything on the beam in Washington?" Ross asked anxiously.

"Yes, with the help of the association's legal department. Got some papers for each of you to sign. Let's not stand here beating our gums. Ross, you and I start on the shield right away. After we eat."

"Good enough."

Ross and the doctor spent three days on the hard, dirty

task of tearing out the fuel system to the tail jets. The nose and belly jets, used only in maneuvering and landing, were left unchanged. These operated on aniline-and-nitric fuel; Cargraves wanted them left as they were, to get around one disadvantage of atomic propulsion—the relative difficulty in turning the power off and on when needed.

As they worked, they brought each other up to date. Ross told him about the man who had tangled with a dud land mine. Cargraves paid little attention until Ross told him about the crates that had been opened. Cargraves laid down his tools and wiped sweat from his face. "I want the details on that," he stated.

"What's the matter, Doc? Nothing was hurt."

"You figure the dead man had been breaking into the stuff?"

"Well, I thought so until I remembered that the Ranger had said flatly that this bozo was already buzzard meat before our stuff arrived."

Cargraves looked worried and stood up. "Where to, Doc?"

"You go ahead with the job," the scientist answered absently. "I've got to see Art." Ross started to speak, thought better of it, and went back to work.

"Art," Cargraves started in, "what are you and Morrie doing now?"

"Why, we're going over his astrogation instruments. I'm tracing out the circuits on the acceleration integrator. The gyro on it seems to be off center, by the way."

"It has to be. Take a look in the operation manual. But never mind that. Could you rig an electric-eye circuit around this place?"

"I could if I had the gear."

"Never mind what you might do 'if'—what can you do with the stuff you've got?"

"Wait a minute, Uncle Don," the younger partner protested. "Tell me what you want to do—I'll tell you if I can wangle it."

"Sorry. I want a prowler circuit around the ship and cabin. Can you do it?"

Art scratched his ear. "Let me see. I'd need photo-electric cells and an ultraviolet light. The rest I can piece together. I've got two light meters in my photo kit; I could rig them for the cells, but I don't know about UV light. If we had a sun lamp, I could filter it. How about an arc? I could jimmy up an arc."

Cargraves shook his head. "Too uncertain. You'd have to stay up all night nursing it. What else can you do?"

"Mmmm. . . . Well, we could use thermocouples maybe. Then I could use an ordinary floodlight and filter it down to infra-red."

"How long would it take? Whatever you do, it's got to be finished by dark, even if it's only charging the top wire of the fence."

"Then I'd better do just that," Art agreed, "if that— Say!"

"Say what?"

"Instead of giving the fence a real charge and depending on shocking anybody that touches it, I'll just push a volt or two through it and hook it back in through an audio circuit with plenty of gain. I can rig it so that if anybody touches the fence it will howl like a dog. How's that?"

"That's better. I want an alarm right now. Get hold of Morrie and both of you work on it." Cargraves went back to his work, but his mind was not on it. The misgivings which he had felt at the time of the mystery of the missing 'blunt instrument' were returning. Now more mysteries—his orderly mind disliked mysteries.

He started to leave the rocket about an hour later to see how Art was making out. His route led him through the hold into the pilot compartment. There he found Morrie. His eyebrows went up. "Hi, sport," he said. "I thought you were helping Art."

Morrie looked sheepish. "Oh, that!" he said. "Well, he did say something about it. But I was busy." He indicated the computer, its cover off.

"Did he tell you I wanted you to help him?"

"Well, yes—but he didn't need my help. He can do that sort of work just as well alone."

Cargraves sat down. "Morrie," he said slowly, "I think we had better have a talk. Have you stopped to think who is going to be second-in-comand of this expedition?"

Morrie did not answer. Cargraves went on. "It has to be you, of course. You're the other pilot. If anything happens to me the other two will have to obey you. You realize that?"

"Art won't like that." Morrie's voice was a mutter.

"Not as things stand now. Art's got his nose out of joint. You can't blame him—he was disappointed that he didn't get to take pilot training, too."

"But that wasn't my fault."

"No, but you've got to fix it. You've got to behave so that, if the time comes, they'll *want* to take your orders. This trip is no picnic. There will be times when our lives may depend on instant obedience. I put it to you bluntly, Morrie—if I had had a choice I would have picked Ross for my second-in-command—he's less flighty than you are. But you're it, and you've got to live up to it. Otherwise we don't take off."

"Oh, we've got to take off! We can't give up now!"

"We'll make it. The trouble is, Morrie," he went on, "American boys are brought up loose and easy. That's fine. I like it that way. But there comes a time when loose and easy isn't enough, when you have to be willing to obey, and do it wholeheartedly and without argument. See what I'm driving at?"

"You mean you want me to get on back to the shop and help Art."

"Correct." He swung the boy around and faced him toward the door, slapped him on the back and said, "Now git!"

Morrie "got." He paused at the door and flung back over his shoulder, "Don't worry about me, Doc. I can straighten out and fly right."

"Roger!" Cargraves decided to have a talk with Art later.

VI   DANGER IN THE DESERT

THE SPACE SUITS WERE delivered the next day, causing another break in the work, to Cargraves' annoyance. However, the boys were so excited over this evidence that they were actually preparing to walk on the face of the moon that he decided to let them get used to the suits.

The suits were modified pressurized stratosphere suits, as developed for the air forces. They looked like diving suits, but were less clumsy. The helmets were "goldfish bowls" of Plexiglas, laminated with soft polyvinyl-butyral plastic to make them more nearly shatter-proof. There were no heating arrangements. Contrary to popular belief, vacuum of outer space has no temperature; it is neither hot nor cold. Man standing on the airless moon would gain or lose heat only by radiation, or by direct contact with the surface of the moon. As the moon was believed to vary from extreme sub-zero to temperatures hotter than boiling water, Cargraves had ordered thick soles of asbestos for the shoes of the suits and similar pads for the seats of the pants of each suit, so that they could sit down occasionally without burning or freezing. Overgloves of the same material completed the insulation against contact. The suits were so well insulated, as well as air-tight, that body heat more than replaced losses through radiation. Cargraves would have preferred thermostatic control, but such refinements could be left to the pioneers and colonists who would follow after.

Each suit had a connection for an oxygen bottle much

larger and heavier than the jump bottle of an aviator, a bottle much too heavy to carry on earth but not too heavy for the surface of the moon, where weight is only one-sixth that found on earth.

The early stratosphere suits tended to starfish and become rigid, which made the simplest movements an effort. In trying on his own suit, Cargraves was pleased to find that these suits were easy to move around in, even when he had Ross blow him up until the suit was carrying a pressure of three atmospheres, or about forty-five pounds to the square inch. The constant-volume feature, alleged for the de-Camp joints, appeared to be a reality.

Cargraves let them experiment, while seeing to it that as many field tests as possible were made to supplement the manufacturer's laboratory tests. Then the suits were turned over to Art for installation of walky-talky equipment.

The following day the doctor turned all the boys to work on the conversion of the drive mechanism. He was expecting delivery of the atomic fission element, thorium; the anti-radiation shield had to be ready. This shield was constructed of lead, steel, and organic plastic, in an arrangement which his calculations indicated would be most effective in screening the alpha, beta, and gamma radiations and the slippery neutrons, from the forward part of the rocket.

Of these radiations, the gamma are the most penetrating and are much like X-rays. Alpha particles are identical with the nuclei of helium atoms; beta particles are simply electrons moving at extremely high speeds. Neutrons are the electrically uncharged particles which make up much of the mass of most atomic nuclei and are the particles which set off or trigger the mighty explosions of atomic bombs.

All of these radiations are dangerous to health and life.

The thorium drive unit was to be shielded only on the forward side, as radiations escaping to outer space could be ignored. Morrie had landed the rocket with one side facing the cabin, inside the corral. It was now necessary to jack the rocket around until the tubes pointed away from the cabin, so that radiations, after the thorium was in place, would go harmlessly out across the crater of the Doomsday Bomb and, also, so that the rocket would be in position for a captive test run with the exhaust directed away from the cabin.

The jacking-around process was done with hydraulic jacks, muscle, and sweat, in sharp contrast to the easy-appearing, powered manipulation of rockets by dolly and cradle and mobile sling, so familiar a sight on any rocket field. It took all of them until late afternoon. When it was over Cargraves declared a holiday and took them on a long-promised trip into the Doomsday Crater.

This bomb site has been pictured and described so much and the boys were so used to seeing it in the distance that the thrill of being in it was limited. Nevertheless the desolation, the utter deadness, of those miles and miles of frozen, glassy waste made their flesh creep. Cargraves marched ahead, carrying a Geiger radiation counter, of the sort used to prospect for uranium in Canada during the war. This was largely to impress the boys with the necessity for unsleeping watchfulness in dealing with radioactive elements. He did not really expect to hear the warning rattle of danger in the ear phones; the test had been made so long before that the grim lake was almost certainly as harmless as the dead streets of Hiroshima.

But it put them in the mood for the lecture he had in mind. "Now, listen, sports," he started in when they got back, "day after tomorrow the thorium arrives. From then on the holiday is over. This stuff is poison. You've got to remember that all the time."

"Sure," agreed Morrie. "We all know that."

"You know it at the tops of your minds. I want you to know it every minute, way down in your guts. We'll stake out the unshielded area between the ship and the fence. If your hat blows into that stretch, let it stay there, let it rot —but don't go after it!"

Ross looked perturbed. "Wait a second, Doc. Would it

really hurt anything to expose yourself for just a few seconds?"

"Probably not," Cargraves agreed, "provided that were all the dosage you ever got. But we will all get some dosage all the time, even through the shield. Radioactivity accumulates its poisonous effect. Any exposure you can possibly avoid, you *must* avoid. It makes your chances better when you get a dose of it accidentally. Art!"

"Uh? Yes, sir!"

"From now on you are the medical officer. You must see to it that everybody wears his X-ray film all the time—and I mean *all* the time—and his electroscope. I want you to change the films and develop them and check the electroscopes according to the dope in the manual. Complete charts on everything, and report to me each Friday morning—oftener if you find anything outside the limits. Got me?"

"Got you, Doc."

"Besides that, you arrange for blood counts once a week for everybody, over in town."

"I think I could learn to do a blood count myself," Art offered.

"You let the regular medico do it. You've got enough to worry about to keep all the electronic equipment purring along properly. One more thing." He looked around him, waiting to get their full attention.

"If any one shows the possibility of overdosage of radiation, by film or by blood count or whatever, I will have to send him home for treatment. It won't be a case of 'just one more chance.' You are dealing with hard facts here—not me, but natural laws. If you make a mistake, out you go and we'll have to find somebody to take your place."

They all nodded solemnly. Art said, "Doc?"

"Yes?"

"Suppose it's your film that shows the overdosage?"

"Me? Not likely! If it does you can kick me all the way to the gate—I'm afraid of that stuff!

"Just the same," he went on more seriously, "you run the same checks on me as on everybody else. Now let's have supper. I want you and Morrie to do the KP tonight, so that Ross can start his study period right after supper. Ross, you and I are getting up at five, so let's hit the sack early."

"Okay. What's cookin'?"

"Trip into Albuquerque—shopping." He was reluctant to explain. The place had no firearms. They had seemed a useless expense—many a man has spent years in the desert without shooting off anything but his mouth, he had reasoned. As for the dreamed-of trip—what could one shoot on the moon?

But signs of prowlers, even in this fenced and forbidding area, had him nervous. Art's watch-dog fence was tested each night and Art slept with the low power-hum of the hot circuit in his ears; thus far there had been no new alarm. Still he was nervous.

Cargraves was awakened about three A.M. to find Art shaking his shoulder and light pouring in his eyes. "Doc! Doc! Wake up!"

"Huh? Wassamatter?"

"I got a squawk over the loudspeaker."

Cargraves was out of bed at once. They bent over the speaker. "I don't hear anything."

"I've got the volume low, but you'd hear it. There it is again—get it?" There had been an unmistakable squawk from the box. "Shall I wake the others?"

"Mmmm . . . no. Not now. Why did you turn on the light?"

"I guess I wanted it," Art admitted.

"I see." Cargraves hauled on trousers and fumbled with his shoes. "I want you to turn out the lights for ten seconds. I'm going out that window. If I'm not back in twenty minutes, or if you hear anything that sounds bad, wake the boys and come get me. But stay together. Don't separate for any reason." He slipped a torch in his pocket. "Okay."

"You ought not to go by yourself."

"Now, Art. I thought we had settled such matters."

"Yes, but—oh, well!" Art posted himself at the switch.

Cargraves was out the window and had cat-footed it

around behind the machine shop before the light came on again. He lurked in the shadow and let his eyes get used to the darkness.

It was a moonless night, clear and desert sharp. Orion blazed in the eastern sky. Cargraves soon was able to pick out the sage bushes, the fence posts, the gloomy bulk of the ship a hundred yards away.

The padlock on the machine shop was undisturbed and the shop's windows were locked. Doing his best to take advantage of the scanty cover, he worked his way down to the ship.

The door was ajar. He could not remember whether he or Ross had been last man out. Even if it had been Ross, it was not like Ross to fail to lock the door.

He found that he was reluctant to enter the craft. He wished that he had not put off buying guns; a forty-five in his hand would have comforted him.

He swung the door open and scrambled in fast, ducking quickly away from the door, where his silhouette would make a target. He crouched in the darkness, listening and trying to slow his pounding heart. When he was sure he could hear nothing, he took the flashlight, held it at arm's length away from him and switched it on.

The piloting compartment was empty. Somewhat relieved, he sneaked back through the hold, empty also, and into the drive compartment. Empty. Nothing seemed disturbed.

He left the ship cautiously, this time making sure that the door was locked. He made a wide sweep around the cabin and machine shop and tried to assure himself that no one was inside the corral. But in the starlight, fifty men might have hidden in the sage, simply by crouching down and holding still.

He returned to the cabin, whistling to Art as he approached.

"About time you got back," Art complained. "I was just about to roust out the others and come and get you. Find anything?"

"No. Anything more out of the squawk box?"

"Not a peep."

"Could it have been a coyote brushing against the wire?"

"How would a coyote get through the outer fence?" Art wanted to know.

"Dig under it. There *are* coyotes in here. We've heard them."

"You can't tell how far a coyote is from you by its howl."

"Listen to the old desert rat! Well, leave the light on, but go back to bed. I'll be awake. I've got to be up in another hour in any case. Crawl in the sack." Cargraves settled down to a pipe and some thought.

Cargraves was too busy on the trip to Albuquerque to worry about the preceding night. Ross's style of herding his hot rod left little time to think about anything but the shortness of life and the difficulty of hanging on to his hat. But Ross poured them into the city with plenty of time for shopping.

Cargraves selected two Garand rifles, Army surplus stock at a cheap price, and added a police thirty-eight special, on a forty-five frame. His mouth watered at a fancy sporting rifle with telescopic sights, but money was getting short; a few more emergency purchases or any great delay in starting would bankrupt the firm.

He ordered a supply of army-style C-rations and K-rations for the trip. Ross remarked privately, while the clerk wrote up the order, "In most stories about space travel, they just eat pills of concentrated food. Do you think it will ever come to that?"

"Not with my money," the physicist answered. "You guys can eat pills if you want to. I want food I can get my teeth in."

"Check," said Ross.

They stopped at a nursery where Cargraves ordered three dozen young rhubarb plants. He planned to use a balanced oxygen-carbon-dioxide air-refreshing system during the stay on the moon, if possible, and the plants were to supply the plant-life half of the cycle. Enough liquid oxygen would be carted along for breathing throughout the round trip, but a "balanced aquarium" arrangement for renewing their air supply would enable them to stay on the moon as long as their food lasted.

The chemical fertilizers needed for hydroponic farming of the rhubarb were ordered also. This done, they grabbed a chocolate malt and a hamburger apiece and high-tailed it for the camp.

Morrie and Art swarmed out of the machine shop as they arrived. "Hi, Doc! Hi, Ross! What's the good word?"

Ross showed them the guns. Art was eager to try them and Cargraves okayed it. Morrie hung back and said, "By the way, Doc, the CAB inspector was here today."

"The what?"

"The Civil Aeronautics inspector. He had a letter from you."

"From me? What did it say?"

"Why, it requested them to send an inspector to go over the rebuilt parts of the rocket and approve it for flight. I told him it wasn't ready."

"What else did you say? Did you tell him it was atomic-powered?"

"No, but he seemed to know it. He knew that we planned a space flight, too. What's the pitch, Doc? I thought you were going to keep it quiet a while longer?"

"So did I," Cargraves said bitterly. "What *did* you tell him?"

"Nothing—so help me. I decided you ought to handle it, so I played stupid. I tipped Art and he did the same. Did we do wrong?" he went on anxiously. "I know he was CAB, but it seemed to me he ought to talk to you. Do you suppose we offended him?"

"I hope you gave him apoplexy," Cargraves said savagely. "He was no CAB inspector, Morrie. He was a phony."

"Huh? Why. . . . But he had your letter."

"Faked. I'll bet he's been holed up somewhere outside the gate, waiting for me to be away. Did you leave him alone at any time?"

"No. Wait a minute—only once, for about five minutes.

61

We were down at the ship and he sent me back for a flashlight. I'm sorry." The boy looked miserable.

"Forget it. It was the natural, polite thing to do. You didn't know he was phony. I wonder how he got through the gate? Did he come in a car?"

"Yes. I . . . Was the gate locked?"

"Yes, but he might have bulldozed the forester into letting him in." They had been moving down toward the ship as they talked. Cargraves made a quick examination of the ship, but found nothing amiss. It seemed likely that the intruder had not found what he was looking for, probably because the drive was not yet installed.

He still worried about the matter of the locked gate. "I'm going to run down to the gate," he announced, heading for the car. "Tell the boys."

"I'll drive you." None of the boys approved the way Cargraves drove a car; it was one respect in which they did not look up to him. Privately, they considered his style stuffy.

"Okay. Snap it up." Morrie ran down toward where the other two were wasting ammunition on innocent tin cans and bellowed at them. Seconds later he had the engine revved up and was ready to gun the rig when Cargraves slid into the seat beside him.

The padlock was intact, but one link of the bullchain had been hack-sawed away and replaced with wire. "So that's that," Cargraves dismissed the matter.

"Hadn't we better put on a new chain?" inquired Morrie.

"Why bother? He's still got the hacksaw."

The trip back was gloomy. Cargraves was worried. Morrie felt responsible for not having unmasked and made prisoner the impostor. In retrospect he could think of a dozen dramatic ways to have done it.

Cargraves told him to keep his lip buttoned until after supper. When the dishes were out of the way, he brought the others up to date on the ominous happenings. Art and Ross took it with grave faces but without apparent excitement. "So that's how it is," Ross said. "Seems like somebody doesn't like us."

"Why that dirty so-and-so," Art said softly. "I thought he was too smooth. I'd like to have him on the other end of one of those Garands."

"Maybe you will," Cargraves answered him soberly. "I might as well admit, fellows, that I've been worried. . . ."

"Shucks, we knew that when you ordered that watch-dog hook-up."

"I suppose so. I can't figure out *why* anybody would do this. Simple curiosity I can understand, once the fact leaked out—as it seems to have done—that we are after space flight. But whoever it is has more than curiosity eating him, considering the lengths he is willing to go to."

"I'll bet he wants to steal your space drive, Uncle Don."

"That would make a swell adventure yarn, Art, but it doesn't make sense. If he knows I've got a rocket drive, all he has to do is apply for a license to the commission and use it."

"Maybe he thinks you are holding out some secrets on the commission?"

"If he thinks so, he can post a bond for the costs and demand an examination. He wouldn't have to fake letters, or bust open gates. If he proves it on me, I go to jail."

"The point is," Morrie asserted, "not why he's snooping but what we can do to stop him. I think we ought to stand watches at night." He glanced at the two rifles.

"No," Cargraves disagreed. "Art's squawk circuit is better than a guard. You can't see enough at night. I found that out."

"Say," put in Art. "Look—I could take the pilot radar and mount it on the roof of the cabin. With it set to scan for a landing it'll pick up anything in the neighborhood."

"No," Cargraves answered. "I wouldn't want to risk jim-mying up the equipment. It's more important to have it just right for the moon landing than it is to use it for prowlers."

"Oh, I won't hurt it!"

"I still think," insisted Morrie, "that getting a shot at him is the best medicine."

"So much the better," Art pointed out. "I'll spot him in

the 'scope. You wear phones with about a thousand feet of cord and I'll coach you right up to him, in the dark. Then you got 'im."

"Sounds good," Morrie agreed.

"Take it easy," Cargraves cautioned. "You fellows may think this is the Wild West but you will find that a judge will take a very sour attitude if you plug a man engaged in simple trespass. You boys've read too many comic books."

"I never touch the things," Art denied fiercely. "Anyhow, not often," he amended.

"If we can't shoot, then why did you buy the guns?" Ross wanted to know.

"Fair enough. You *can* shoot—but you have to be certain it's self-defense; I'll take those guns back to the shop before I'll have a bunch of wild men running around with blood in their eyes and an itch in their trigger fingers. The other use for the guns is to throw a scare into any more prowlers. You can shoot, but shoot where he *isn't*—unless he shoots first."

"Okay." "Suits." "I hope he shoots first!"

"Any other ideas?"

"Just one," Art answered. "Suppose our pal cut our power line. We've got everything on it—light, radio, even the squawk box. He could cut the line after we went to sleep and loot the whole place without us knowing it."

Cargraves nodded. "I should have thought of that." He considered it. "You and I will string a temporary line right now from the ship's batteries to your squawk box. Tomorrow we'll hook up an emergency lighting circuit." He stood up. "Come on, Art. And you guys get busy. Study hour."

"Study hour?" Ross protested. "Tonight? We can't keep our minds on books—not tonight."

"You can make a stab at it," the doctor said firmly. "Guys have been known to write books while waiting to be hanged."

The night passed quietly. Ross and Doc were down at the ship early the next morning, leaving Art and Morrie to work out an emergency lighting circuit from the battery of the car. Doc planned to have everything ready for the thorium when it arrived. He and Ross climbed into the rocket and got cheerfully to work. Cargraves started laying out tools, while Ross, whistling merrily off key, squeezed himself around the edge of the shield.

Cargraves looked up just in time to see a bright, bright flash, then to be hit in the face by a thunderous pressure which threw him back against the side of the ship.

VII "WE'LL GO IF WE HAVE TO WALK"

ART WAS SHAKING HIS SHOULDER. "Doc!" he was pleading. "Doc! Wake up—are you hurt bad?"

"Ross . . ." Cargraves said vaguely.

"It's not Ross; it's Art."

"But Ross—how's Ross? Did it, did it kill him?"

"I don't know. Morrie's with him."

"Go find out."

"But you're——"

"Go find out, I said!" Whereupon he passed out again.

When he came to a second time, Art was bending over him. "Uncle," he said, "the thorium has come. What do we do?"

Thorium. Thorium? His head ached, the word seemed to have no meaning. "Uh, I'll be out in a . . . what about Ross? Is he dead?"

"No, he's not dead."

"How bad is he hurt?"

"It seems to be his eyes, mostly. He isn't cut up any, but

he can't see. What'll I tell them about the thorium, Uncle?"

"Oh, hang the thorium! Tell them to take it back."

"*What?*"

He tried to get up, but he was too dizzy, too weak. He let his head fall back and tried to collect his spinning thoughts. "Don't be a dope, Art," he muttered peevishly. "We don't need thorium. The trip is off, the whole thing was a mistake. Send it back—it's poison." His eyes were swimming; he closed them. "Ross . . ." he said.

He was again brought back to awareness by the touch of hands on his body. Morrie and Art were gently but firmly going over him. "Take it easy, Doc," Morrie warned him.

"Well . . ." Morrie wrinkled his brow. "Ross seems all right, except for his eyes. He says he's all right."

"But he's blind?"

"Well, he can't see."

"We've got to get him to a hospital." Cargraves sat up and tried to stand up. "Ow!" He sat down suddenly.

"It's his foot," said Art.

"Let's have a look at it. Hold still, Doc." They took his left shoe off gently and peeled back the sock. Morrie felt it over. "What do you think, Art?"

Art examined it. "It's either a sprain or a break. We'll have to have an X-ray."

"Where's Ross?" Cargraves persisted. "We've got to get him to a hospital."

"Sure, sure," Morrie agreed. "We've got to get you to one, too. We moved Ross up to the cabin."

"I want to see him."

"Comin' up! Half a sec, while I get the car."

With Art's help Cargraves managed to get up on his good foot and hobble to the door. Getting down from the ship's door was painful, but he made it, and fell thankfully into the seat of the car.

"Who's there?" Ross called out, as they came in with Cargraves leaning on the two boys.

"All of us," Art told him.

Cargraves saw that Ross was lying in his bunk with his

eyes covered with a handkerchief. Cargraves hobbled over to him. "How is it, kid?" he said huskily.

"Oh, it's you, Doc. I'll get by. It'll take more than that to do me in. How are you?"

"I'm all right. How about your eyes?"

"Well," Ross admitted, "to tell the truth, they don't work too well. All I see is purple and green lights." He kept his voice steady, almost cheerful, but the pulse in his neck was throbbing visibly. Cargraves started to remove the bandage. Morrie stopped him.

"Let the bandage alone, Doc," he said firmly. "There's nothing to see. Wait till we get him to a hospital."

"But . . . Okay, okay. Let's get on with it."

"We were just waiting for you. Art will drive you."

"What are you going to do?"

"I," said Morrie, "am going to climb up on the roof of this shack with a load of sandwiches and a gun. I'll still be there when you get back."

"But—" Cargraves shrugged and let the matter pass.

Morrie scrambled down when they got back and helped Cargraves hobble into the cabin. Ross was led in by Art; his eyes were bandaged professionally and a pair of dark glasses stuck out of his shirt pocket. "What's the score?" Morrie demanded of all of them, but his eyes were fastened on Ross.

"It's too early to tell," Cargraves said heavily, as he eased into a chair. "No apparent damage, but the optic nerve seems paralyzed."

Morrie clucked and said nothing. Ross groped at a chair and sat down. "Relax," he advised Morrie. "I'll be all right. The flash produced a shock in the eyes. The doctor told me all about it. Sometimes a case like this goes on for three months or so, then it's all right."

Cargraves bit his lip. The doctor had told him more than he had told Ross; sometimes it was not all right; sometimes it was permanent.

"How about you, Doc?"

"Sprain, and a wrenched back. They strapped me up."

"Nothing else?"

"No. Anti-tetanus shots for both of us, but that was just to be on the safe side."

"Well," Morrie announced cheerfully, "it looks to me as if the firm would be back in production in short order."

"No," Cargraves denied. "No, it won't be. I've been trying to tell these goons something ever since we left the hospital, but they wouldn't listen. We're through. The firm is busted."

None of the boys said anything. He went on, raising his voice. "There won't be any trip to the moon. Can't you see that?"

Morrie looked at him impassively. "You said, 'The firm is busted.' You mean you're out of money?"

"Well, not quite, but that's a factor. What I meant——"

"I've got some E-bonds," Ross announced, turning his bandaged head.

"That's not the point," Cargraves answered, with great gentleness. "I appreciate the offer; don't think I don't. And don't think I want to give up. But I've had my eyes opened. It was foolish, foolish from the start, sheer folly. But I let my desires outweigh my judgment. I had no business getting you kids into this. Your father was right, Ross. Now I've got to do what I can to make amends."

Ross shook his head. Morrie glanced at Art and said, "How about it, medical officer?"

Art looked embarrassed, started to speak, and changed his mind. Instead he went to the medicine cabinet, and took out a fever thermometer. He came back to Cargraves. "Open your mouth, Uncle."

Cargraves started to speak. Art popped the tube in his mouth. "Don't talk while I'm taking your temperature," he warned, and glanced at his wrist watch.

"Why, what the——"

"Keep your mouth closed!"

Cargraves subsided, fuming. Nobody said anything until

Art reached again for the thermometer. "What does it say?" Morrie demanded.

"A tenth over a hundred."

"Let me see that," Cargraves demanded. Art held it away from him. The doctor stood up, absent-mindedly putting his weight on his injured foot. He then sat down quite suddenly. Art shook down the thermometer, cleaned it and put it away.

"It's like this," Morrie said firmly. "You aren't boss; I'm boss."

"Huh? What in the world has got into you, Morrie?"

Morrie said, "How about it, Art?"

Art looked embarrassed but said stubbornly, "That's how it is, Uncle."

"Ross?"

"I'm not sure of the pitch," Ross said slowly, "but I see what they are driving at. I'm stringing along with Art and Morrie."

Cargraves' head was beginning to ache again. "I think you've all gone crazy. But it doesn't make any difference; we're washed up anyhow."

"No," Morrie said, "we're not crazy, and it remains to be seen whether or not we're washed up. The point is: you are on the sick list. That puts me in charge; you set it up that way yourself. You can't give any orders or make any decisions for us until you are off the sick list."

"But—" He stopped and then laughed, his first laugh in hours. "This is nuts. You're hijacking me, with a technicality. You can't put me on the sick list for a little over a degree of temperature."

"You weren't put on the sick list for that; you are being kept on the sick list for it. Art put you on the sick list while you were unconscious. You stay there until he takes you off —you made him medical officer."

"Yes, but— Look here, Art—you put me on the sick list earlier? This isn't just a gag you thought up to get around me?"

"No, Uncle," Art assured him, "when I told Morrie that

you said not to accept the thorium, he tried to check with you. But you were out like a light. We didn't know what to do, until Morrie pointed out that I was medical officer and that I had to decide whether or not you were in shape to carry out your job. So——"

"But you don't have. . . . Anyway, all this is beside the point. I sent the thorium back; there isn't going to be any trip; there isn't any medical officer; there isn't any second-in-command. The organization is done with."

"But that's what I've been trying to tell you, Uncle. We didn't send the thorium back."

"Huh?"

"I've signed for it," Morrie explained, "as your agent."

Cargraves rubbed his forehead. "You kids—you beat me! However, it doesn't make any difference. I have made up my mind that the whole idea was a mistake. *I* am not going to the moon and that puts the kibosh on it. Wait a minute, Morrie! I'm not disputing that you are in charge, temporarily—but I can talk, can't I?".

"Sure. You can talk. But nothing gets settled until your temperature is down and you've had a night's sleep."

"Okay. But you'll see that things settle themselves. You have to have me to build the space drive. Right?"

"Mmmm . . . yes."

"No maybes about it. You kids are learning a lot about atomics, fast. But you don't know enough. I haven't even told you, yet, how the drive is supposed to work."

"We could get a license on your patent, even without your permission," Ross put in. "We're going to the moon."

"Maybe you could—if you could get another nuclear physicist to throw in with you. But it wouldn't be this enterprise. Listen to me, kids. Never mind any touch of fever I've got. I'm right in the head for the first time since I got banged on the head at your rocket test. And I want to explain some things. We've got to bust up, but I don't want you sore at me."

"What do you mean: 'since you got banged on the head'?"

Cargraves spoke very soberly. "I knew at that time, after

we looked over the grounds, that that 'accident' was no accident. Somebody put a slug on me, probably with a blackjack. I couldn't see why then and I still don't see why. I should have seen the light when we started having prowlers. But I couldn't believe that it was really serious. Yesterday I knew it was. Nobody impersonates a federal inspector unless he's playing for high stakes and willing to do almost anything. It had me worried sick. But I still didn't see why anybody would want anything we've got and I certainly didn't think they would try to kill us."

"You think they meant to kill us?" asked Ross.

"Obviously. The phony inspector booby-trapped us. He planted some sort of a bomb."

"Maybe he meant to wreck the ship rather than to kill us."

"What for?"

"Well," said Art, "maybe they're after the senior prizes."

"Wrecking our ship won't win him any prize money."

"No, but it could keep us from beating him."

"Maybe. It's far-fetched but it's as good an answer as any. But the reason doesn't matter. Somebody is out to get us and he's willing to go to any lengths. This desert is a lonely place. If I could afford a squadron of guards around the place we might bull it through. But I can't. And I can't let you kids get shot or bombed. It's not fair to you, nor to your parents."

Art looked stubborn and unhappy. Morrie's face was an impassive mask. Finally he said, "If that's all you've got to say, Doc, I suggest we eat and adjourn until tomorrow."

"All right."

"Not just yet." Ross had stood up. He groped for the back of his chair and tried to orient himself. "Where are you, Doc?"

"I'm here—to your left."

"All right. Now I've got some things to say. I'm going to the moon. I'm going to the moon, somehow, whether you want to go or not. I'm going to the moon even if I never get back the use of my eyes. I'm going to the moon even if

71

Morrie or Art has to lead me around. You can do as you please.

"But I'm surprised at you, Doc," he went on. "You're afraid to take the responsibility for us, aren't you? That's the size of it?"

"Yes, Ross, that's the size of it."

"Yet you were willing to take the responsibility of leading us on a trip to the moon. That's more dangerous than anything that could happen here, isn't it? Isn't it?"

Cargraves bit his lip. "It's different."

"I'll tell you how it's different. If we get killed trying to make the jump, ninety-nine chances out of a hundred we all get killed together. You don't have to go back and explain anything to our parents. That's how it's different!"

"Now, Ross!"

"Don't 'Now, Ross' me. What the deuce, Doc?" he went on bitterly. "Suppose it had happened on the moon: would you be twittering around, your morale all shot? Doc, I'm surprised at you. If you are going to have an attack of nerves every time the going gets a little tough, I vote for Morrie for permanent captain."

"That's about enough, Ross," Morrie put in quietly.

"Okay. I was through, anyway." Ross sat down.

There was an uncomfortable silence. Morrie broke it by saying, "Art, let's you and me throw together some food. Study hour will be late as it is." Cargraves looked surprised. Morrie saw his expression and continued. "Sure. Why not? Art and I can take turns reading aloud."

Cargraves pretended to be asleep that night long before he was. Thus he was able to note that Morrie and Art stood alternate watches all night, armed and ready. He refrained from offering any advice.

The boys both went to bed at sunrise. Cargraves got painfully but quietly out of bed and dressed. Leaning on a stick he hobbled down to the ship. He wanted to inspect the damage done by the bomb, but he noticed first the case containing the thorium, bulking large because of its anti-radiation shipping shield. He saw with relief that the seal of the atomics commission was intact. Then he hunched himself inside the ship and made his way slowly to the drive compartment.

The damage was remarkably light. A little welding, he thought, some swaging, and some work at the forge would fix it. Puzzled, he cautiously investigated further.

He found six small putty-like pieces of a plastic material concealed under the back part of the shield. Although there were no primers and no wiring attached to these innocent-appearing little objects he needed no blueprint to tell him what they were. It was evident that the saboteur had not had time to wire more than one of his deadly little toys in the few minutes he had been alone. His intentions had certainly been to wreck the drive compartment—and kill whoever was unlucky enough to set off the trap.

With great care, sweating as he did so, he removed the chunks of explosive, then searched carefully for more. Satisfied, he slipped them into his shirt pocket and went outside. The scramble, hampered by his game leg, out of the door of the rocket, made him shaky; he felt like a human bomb. Then he limped to the corral fence and threw them as far as he could out into the already contaminated fields. He took the precaution of removing them all from his person before throwing the first one, as he wanted to be ready to fall flat. But there was no explosion; apparently the stuff was relatively insensitive to shock. Finished, he turned away, content to let sun and rain disintegrate the stuff.

He found Ross outside the cabin, turning his bandaged face to the morning sun. "That you, Doc?" the young man called out.

"Yes. Good morning, Ross."

"Good morning, Doc." Ross moved toward the scientist, feeling the ground with his feet. "Say, Doc—I said some harsh things last night. I'm sorry. I was upset, I guess."

"Forget it. We are all upset." He found the boy's groping hand and pressed it. "How are your eyes?"

Ross's face brightened. "Coming along fine. I slipped a peek under the bandage when I got up. I can see——"

"Good!"

"I can see, but everything's fuzzy and I see double, or maybe triple. But the light hurt my eyes so I put the bandage back."

"It sounds as if you were going to be all right," Cargraves ventured. "But take it easy."

"Oh, I will. Say, Doc . . ."

"Yes, Ross?"

"Nnnn . . . oh, nothing. Never mind."

"I think I know, Ross. I've changed my mind. I changed my mind last night before I got to sleep. We're going through with it."

"Good!"

"Maybe it's good, maybe it's bad. I don't know. But if that's the way you fellows feel about it, I'm with you. We'll go if we have to walk."

VIII SKYWARD!

"THAT SOUNDS MORE LIKE you, Doc!"

"Thanks. Are the others up yet?"

"Not yet. They didn't get much sleep."

"I know. Let's let them sleep. We'll sit out in the car. Take my arm."

When they had settled themselves Ross asked, "Doc, how much longer will it take to get ready?"

"Not long. Why?"

"Well, I think the key to our problems lies in how fast we can get away. If these attempts to stop us keep up, one of them is going to work. I wish we would leave today."

"We can't do that," Cargraves answered, "but it shouldn't be long. First I've got to install the drive, but it's really just a matter of fitting the parts together. I had almost everything prepared before I ever laid eyes on you guys."

"I wish my blinkers weren't on the fritz."

"It's one job I'll have to do myself. Not that I am trying to keep you out of it, Ross," he added hastily, seeing the boy's expression. "I've never explained it because I thought it would be easier when we had all the gear in front of us."

"Well, how does it work?"

"You remember Heron's turbine in elementary physics? Little boiler on the bottom and a whirligig like a lawn sprinkler on top? You heat the boiler, steam comes up through the whirligig, and makes it whirl around. Well, my drive works like that. Instead of fire, I use a thorium atomic power pile; instead of water, I use zinc. We boil the zinc, vaporize it, get zinc 'steam.' We let the 'steam' exhaust through the jet. That's the works."

Ross whistled. "Simple—and neat. But will it work?"

"I know it'll work. I was trying for a zinc 'steam' power plant when I hit on it. I got the hard, hot jet I wanted, but I couldn't get the turbine to stand up under it. Broke all the blades. Then I realized I had a rocket drive."

"It's slick, Doc! But say—why don't you use lead? You'd get more mass with less bulk."

"A good point. Concentrated mass means a smaller rocket motor, smaller tanks, smaller ship, less dead weight all around. But mass isn't our main trouble; what we've got to have is a high-velocity jet. I used zinc because it has a lower boiling point than lead. I want to superheat the vapor so as to get a good, fast jet, but I can't go above the stable limit of the moderator I'm using."

"Carbon?"

"Yes, carbon—graphite. We use carbon to moderate the

75

neutron flow and cadmium inserts to control the rate of operation. The radiations get soaked up in a bath of liquid zinc. The zinc boils and the zinc 'steam' goes whizzing out the jet as merry as can be."

"I see. But why don't you use mercury instead of zinc? It's heavier than lead and has a lower boiling point than either one of them."

"I'd like to, but it's too expensive. This is strictly a cut-rate show." Doc broke off as Morrie stuck his head out the cabin door.

"Hi, there! Come to breakfast, or we'll throw it out!"

"Don't do that!" Cargraves slipped a leg over the side of the car—the wrong leg—touched the ground and said, "Ouch!"

"Wait a minute, and lean on me," Ross suggested.

They crept back, helping each other. "Aside from the pile," Cargraves went on, "there isn't much left. The thorium is already imbedded in the graphite according to my calculations. That leaves just two major jobs: the air lock and a test-stand run."

The rocket, although it had operated on the trans-Atlantic run above the atmosphere, had no air lock, since its designers had never intended it to be opened up save on the ground. If they were to walk the face of the moon, an air lock, a small compartment with two doors, was necessary. Cargraves planned to weld a steel box around the inside of the present door frame, with a second air-tight door, opening inward.

"I can weld the lock," Ross offered, "while you rig the pile. That is, if my eyes clear up in time."

"Even if they do, I don't think it would be smart to stare at a welding arc. Can't the others weld?"

"Well, yes, but just between us chickens, I run a smoother seam."

"We'll see."

At breakfast Cargraves told the other two of his decision to go ahead. Art turned pink and got his words twisted.

Morrie said gravely, "I thought your temperature would go down over night. What are the plans?"

"Just the same, only more so. How's your department?"

"Shucks, I could leave this afternoon. The gyros are purring like kittens; I've calculated Hohmann orbits and S-trajectories till I'm sick of 'em; the computer and me are like that." He held out two fingers.

"Fine. You concentrate on getting the supplies in, then. How about you, Art?"

"Who, me? Why, I've got everything lined up, I guess. Both radars are right on the beam. I've got a couple wrinkles I'd like to try with the FM circuit."

"Is it all right the way it is?"

"Good enough, I guess."

"Then don't monkey with the radios. I can keep you busy."

"Oh, sure."

"How about the radar screen Art was going to rig?" Morrie inquired.

"Eh? Oh, you mean the one for our friend the prowler. Hm. . . ." Cargraves studied the matter. "Ross thinks and I agree that the best way to beat the prowler is to get out of here as fast as we can. I don't want that radar out of the ship. It would waste time and always with the chance of busting a piece of equipment we can't afford to replace and can't get along without."

Morrie nodded. "Suits. I still think that a man with a gun in his hands is worth more than a gadget anyhow. See here—there are four of us. That's two hours a night. Let's stand guard."

Cargraves agreed to this. Various plans were offered to supplement the human guard and the charged fence, but all were voted down as too time-consuming, too expensive or impractical. It was decided to let the matter stand, except that lights would be left burning at night, including a string to be rigged around the ship. All of these lines were to be wired to cut over automatically to the ship's batteries.

Cargraves sat down to lunch on Wednesday of the following week with a feeling of satisfaction. The thorium power pile was in place, behind the repaired shield. This in itself was good; he disliked the finicky, ever-dangerous work of handling the radioactive element, even though he used body shields and fished at it with tongs.

But the pile was built; the air lock had been welded in place and tested for air-tightness; almost all the supplies were aboard. Acceleration hammocks had been built for Art and Ross (Cargraves and Morrie would ride out the surges of power in the two pilot seats). The power pile had been operated at a low level; all was well, he felt, and the lights on the board were green.

The phony inspector had not showed up again, nor were the night watches disturbed. Best of all, Ross's eyesight had continued to improve; the eye specialist had pronounced him a cure on Monday, subject to wearing dark glasses for a couple of weeks.

Cargraves' sprain still made him limp, but he had discarded his stick. Nothing bothered him. He tackled *Aggregate à la Galileo* (hash to ordinary mortals) with enthusiasm, while thinking about a paper he would write for the *Physical Review. Some Verified Experimental Factors in Space Flight* seemed like a good title—by Doctor Donald Morris Cargraves, B.S., Sc.D., LL.D., Nobel Prize, Nat. Adad., Fr. Acad., etc. The honors were not yet his—he was merely trying them on for size.

The car ground to a stop outside and Art came in with the mail. "Santa Claus is here!" he greeted them. "One from your folks, Ross, and one from that synthetic blonde you're sweet on."

"I'm not sweet on her and she's a natural blonde," Ross answered emphatically.

"Have it your own way—you'll find out. Three for you, Morrie—all business. The rest are yours, Doc," he finished, holding back the one from his mother. "Hash again," he added.

"It's to soften you up for what you're going to eat on the moon," said the cook. "Say, Doc——"

"Yes, Morrie?"

"The canned rations are at the express office in town, it says here. I'll pick 'em up this afternoon. The other two are bills. That finishes my check-off list."

"Good," he answered absently, as he tore open a letter. "You can help Ross and me on the test stand. That's the only big job left." He unfolded the letter and read it.

Then he reread it. Presently Ross noticed that he had stopped eating and said, "What's the matter, Doc?"

"Well, nothing much, but it's awkward. The Denver out-fit can't supply the dynamometers for the test stand run." He tossed the letter to Ross.

"How bad off does that leave us?" asked Morrie.

"I don't know, yet. I'll go with you into town. Let's make it right after lunch; I have to call the East Coast and I don't want to get boxed in by the time difference."

"Can do."

Ross handed the letter back. "Aren't there plenty of other places to buy them?"

"Hardly 'plenty.' Half-a-million-pound dynamometers aren't stock items. We'll try Baldwin Locomotives."

"Why don't we make them?" asked Art. "We made our own for the *Starstruck* series."

Cargraves shook his head. "High as my opinion is of you lugs as good, all-around jack-leg mechanics and pretzel benders, some jobs require special equipment. But speaking of the *Starstruck* series," he went on, intentionally changing the subject, "do you guys realize we've never named the ship? How does *Starstruck VI* appeal to you?"

Art liked it. Morrie objected that it should be *Moonstruck*. But Ross had another idea. "*Starstruck* was a good enough name for our model rockets, but we want something with a little more—oh, I don't know; dignity, I guess—for the moon ship."

"The *Pioneer*?" "Corny." "The *Thor*—for the way she's powered." "Good, but not enough." "Let's call it the *Einstein*."

"I see why you want to name it for Doctor Einstein," Cargraves put in, "but maybe I've got another name that will symbolize the same thing to you. How about the *Galileo?*"

There was no dissension; the members of the Galileo Club again were unanimous. The man who had first seen and described the mountains of the moon, the man whose very name had come to stand for steadfast insistence on scientific freedom and the freely inquiring mind—his name was music to them.

Cargraves wondered whether or not their own names would be remembered after more than three centuries. With luck, with lots of luck—Columbus had not been forgotten. If the luck ran out, well, a rocket crash was a fast clean death.

The luck appeared to be running out, and with nothing as gallant and spectacular as a doomed and flaming rocket. Cargraves sweated in a phone booth until after five o'clock, East Coast time, and then another hour until it was past five in Chicago as well before he admitted that dynamometers of the size he needed were not to be had on short notice.

He blamed himself for having slipped up, while neglecting to credit himself with having planned to obtain the instruments from the Denver firm for reasons of economy; he had expected to get them second-hand. But blaming himself comforted him.

Morrie noted his long face as he climbed into the heavily loaded little car. "No soap, eh?"

"No soap. Let's get back to camp."

They sped along the desert road in worried silence for several minutes. Finally Morrie spoke up. "How about this, Doc? Make a captive run on the ground with the same yoke and frame you planned to use, but without dynamometers."

"What good would that do? I have to know what the thrust is."

"I'm getting to that. We put a man inside. He watches the accelerometer—the pendulum accelerometer of course; not the distance-integrating one. It read in g's. Figure the number of gravities against the gross weight of the ship at the time and you come out with your thrust in pounds."

Cargraves hesitated. The boy's mistake was so obvious and yet so easy to make that he wished to point it out without hurting his pride. "It's a clever plan, except that I would want to use remote control—there's always the chance that a new type of atomic-fission power plant will blow up. But that's not the hitch; if the ship is anchored to the ground, it won't be accelerating no matter how much thrust is developed."

"Oh!" said Morrie. "Hmm. I sure laid an egg on that one, Doc."

"Natural mistake."

After another five miles Morrie spoke again. "I've got it, Doc. The *Galileo* has to be free to move to show thrust on the accelerometer. Right? Okay, I'll test-fly it. Hold it, hold it," he went on quicky, "I know exactly what you are going to say: you won't let any one take a risk if you can help it. The ship might blow up, or it might crash. Okay, so it might. But it's my job. I'm not essential to the trip; you are. You have to have Ross as flight engineer; you have to have Art for the radar and radio; you don't have to have a second pilot. I'm elected."

Cargraves tried to make his voice sound offhand. "Morrie, your analysis does your heart credit, but not your head. Even if what you said is true, the last part doesn't quite add up. I may be essential, *if* the trip is made. But if the test flight goes wrong, if the power pile blows, or if the ship won't handle and crashes, then there won't be any trip and I'm *not* essential."

Morrie grinned. "You're sharp as a tack, Doc."

"Tried to frame me, eh? Well, I may be old and feeble but I'm not senile. Howsomever, you've given me the answer. We skip the captive run and test-fly it. I test-fly it."

Morrie whistled, "When?"

"Just as soon as we get back."

Morrie pushed the accelerator down to the floor boards; Cargraves wished that he had kept quiet until they reached the camp.

Forty minutes later he was handing out his final instructions. "Drive outside the reservation and find some place at least ten miles away where you can see the camp and where you can huddle down behind a road cut or something. If you see a Hiroshima mushroom, *don't try to come back.* Drive on into town and report to the authorities." He handed Ross a briefcase. "In case I stub my toe, give this stuff to your father. He'll know what to do with it. Now get going. I'll give you twenty minutes. My watch says seven minutes past five."

"Just a minute, Doc."

"What is it, Morrie?" His tones showed nervous irritability.

"I've polled the boys and they agree with me. The *Galileo* is expendable but you aren't. They want you left around to try it again."

"That's enough on that subject, Morrie."

"Well, I'll match you for it."

"You're on thin ice, Morrie!"

"Yes, sir." He climbed in the car. The other two squeezed in beside him. "So long!" "Good luck!"

He waved back at them as they drove away, then turned toward the open door of the *Galileo.* He was feeling suddenly very lonely.

The boys found such a spot and crouched down behind a bank, like soldiers in a trench. Morrie had a small telescope; Art and Ross were armed with the same opera glasses they had used in their model rocket tests. "He's closed the door," announced Morrie.

"What time is it?"

"I've got five twenty-five."

"Any time now. Keep your eyes peeled." The rocket was tiny even through the opera glasses; Morrie's view was slightly better. Suddenly he yelled. "That's it! Geronimo!"

The tail jet, bright silver even in the sun light, had flared out. The ship did not move. "There go his nose jets!" Red and angry, the aniline-and-nitric reached out in front. The *Galileo,* being equipped with nose and belly maneuvering jets, could take off without a launching platform or catapult. He brought his belly jets into play now; the bow of the *Galileo* reared up, but the opposing nose and tail jets kept her nailed to one spot.

"He's off!" The red plumes from the nose were suddenly cut and the ship shot away from the ground. It was over their heads almost before they could catch their breaths. Then it was beyond them and shooting toward the horizon. As it passed over the mountains, out of sight, the three exhaled simultaneously. "Gosh!" said Art, very softly.

Ross started to run. "Hey, where y' going?"

"Back to the camp! We want to be there before he is!"

"Oh!" They tore after him.

Ross set a new high in herding the rig back to the camp site, but his speed did not match their urgency. Nor were they ahead of time. The *Galileo* came pouring back over the horizon and was already braking on her nose jets when the car slammed to a stop.

She came in at a steep dive, with the drive jet already dead. The nose jets splashed the ground on the very spot where she had taken off. He kicked her up with the belly jets and she pancaked in place. Morrie shook his head. "What a landing!" he said reverently.

Cargraves fell out of the door into a small mob. The boys yelled and pounded him on the back.

"How did she behave? How did she handle?"

"Right on the button! The control of the drive jet is logy but we expected that. Once she's hot she doesn't want to cool off. You have to get rid of your head of 'steam.' I was half way to Oklahoma City before I could slow down enough to turn and come back."

"Boy, oh boy! What a ship!"

"When do we start?"

Cargraves' face sobered. "Does staying up all night to pack suit you?"

"Does it! Just try us!"

"It's a deal. Art, get in the ship and get going with the radio. Get the Associated Press station at Salt Lake. Get the United Press. Call up the radio news services. Tell them to get some television pick-ups out here. The lid is off now. Make them realize there is a story here."

"On my way!" He scrambled up into the ship, then paused in the door. "Say—what if they don't believe me?"

"Make them believe you. Tell them to call Doctor Larksbee at the commission for confirmation. Tell them that if they miss they'll be scooped on the biggest story since the war. And say—call up Mr. Buchanan on the forestry frequency. He's kept his mouth shut for us; he ought to be in on it."

By midnight the job was practically complete and Cargraves insisted that they take turns lying down, two at a time, not to sleep, but just to keep from starting the trip completely tired out. The fuel tanks for the belly and nose jets were topped off and the specially installed reserve tanks were filled. The tons of zinc which served the main drive were already aboard as well as an equal weight of powdered reserve. The food was aboard; the carefully rationed water was aboard. (Water was no problem; the air-conditioner would scavenge the vapor of their own exhalations.) The liquid oxygen tanks were full. Cargraves himself had carried aboard the two Garands, excusing it to himself on the pretext that they might land in some wild spot on the return trip . . . that, despite the fact they had ripped the bindings from their few books in order to save space and weight.

He was tired. Only the carefully prepared lists enabled him to be sure that the ship was in all respects ready—or would be soon.

The boys were tired, confused, and excited. Morrie had worked the problem of their departure trajectory three times and then had gotten nerves over it, although it had checked to the last decimal each time. He was gnawed by fear that he had made some silly and fatal mistake and was not satisfied until Cargraves had gotten the same answer, starting with a clear board.

Mr. Buchanan, the Ranger, showed up about one o'clock.

"Is this the Central New Mexico Insane Asylum?" he inquired pleasantly.

Cargraves admitted it. "I've wondered what you folks were up to," the Ranger went on. "Of course I saw your ship, but your message surely surprised me. I hope you don't mind me thinking you're crazy; I wish you luck just the same."

"Thanks." Cargraves showed him the ship, and explained their plans. The moon was full and an hour past its greatest elevation. They planned to take off shortly after daybreak, as it was sinking in the west. This would lose them the earth's spin, but, after the trial run, Cargraves did not care; he had power to throw away. Waiting twelve hours to save a difference of about 1600 miles per hour was more than his nerves could stand.

He had landed the rocket faced west; it would save jacking her around as well.

Buchanan looked the layout over and asked where the jets would splash. Cargraves showed him. Whereupon Buchanan asked, "Have you arranged for any guards?"

In truth, Cargraves had forgotten it. "Never mind," said Buchanan, "I'll call Captain Taylor and get some state police over."

"Never mind calling; we'll radio. Art!"

The press started showing up at four; by the time the state police arrived, Cargraves knew that he had been saved real grief. The place was crowded. Escorts were necessary from the outer gate to the corral to make sure that no one drove on the danger-studded mock-battle fields. Once in the corral it took the firm hand of the state police to keep them there—and to keep them from swarming over the ship.

At five they ate their last breakfast in the camp, with a guard at the door to give them some peace. Cargraves refused to be interviewed; he had prepared a typed handout and given copies to Buchanan to distribute. But the boys were button-holed whenever his back was turned. Finally Captain Taylor assigned a bodyguard to each.

They marched in a hollow square of guards to the ship.

Flash guns dazzled their eyes and television scanners followed their movements. It seemed impossible that this was the same lonely spot where, only hours before, they had worried about silent prowlers in the dark.

Cargraves had the boys climb in, then turned to Buchanan and Captain Taylor. "Ten minutes, gentlemen. Are you sure you can keep everybody clear? Once I get in the seat I can't see the ground near me."

"Don't worry, Captain Cargraves," Taylor assured him. "Ten minutes it is."

Buchanan stuck out his hand. "Good luck, Doctor. Bring me back some green cheese."

A man came puffing up, dodged past a guard, and thrust a folded paper in Cargraves' hand. "Here, what's this?" demanded Taylor. "Get back where you belong."

The man shrugged. "It's a court order."

"Eh? What sort?"

"Temporary injunction against flying this ship. Order to appear and show cause why a permanent injunction should not be issued to restrain him from willfully endangering the lives of minors."

Cargraves stared. It felt to him as if the world were collapsing around him. Ross and Art appeared at the door behind him. "Doc, what's up?"

"Hey, there! You boys—come down out of there," yelled the stranger, and then said to Captain Taylor, "I've got another paper directing me to take them in charge on behalf of the court."

"Get back in the ship," Cargraves ordered firmly, and opened the paper. It seemed in order. State of New Mexico and so forth. The stranger began to expostulate. Taylor took him by the arm.

"Take it easy," he said.

"Thanks," said Cargraves. "Mr. Buchanan, can I have a word with you? Captain, will you hang on to this character?"

"Now, I don't want any beef," protested the stranger. "I'm just carrying out my duty."

"I wonder," Cargraves said thoughtfully. He led Buchanan around the nose of the craft and showed him the paper.

"It seems to be in order," Buchanan admitted.

"Maybe. This says it's the order of a *state* court. This is federal territory, isn't it? As a matter of fact, Captain Taylor and his men are here only by your invitation and consent. Isn't that right?"

"Hmmm . . . yes. That's so." Buchanan suddenly jammed the paper in his pocket. "I'll fix his clock!"

"Just a minute." Cargraves told him rapidly about the phony inspector, and the prowlers, matters which he had kept to himself, save for a letter to the Washington CAB office. "This guy may be a phony, or a stooge of a phony. Don't let him get away until you check with the court that supposedly issued this order."

"I won't!"

They went back, and Buchanan called Taylor aside. Cargraves took the stranger by the arm, not gently. The man protested. "How would you like a poke in the eye?" Cargraves inquired.

Cargraves was six inches taller, and solid. The man shut up. Taylor and Buchanan came back in a moment or two. The state policeman said, "You are due to take off in three minutes, Captain. I had better be sure the crowd is clear." He turned and called out, "Hey! Sergeant Swanson!"

"Yes, sir!"

"Take charge of this guy." It was the stranger, not Cargraves, whom he indicated.

Cargraves climbed in the ship. As he turned to close the door a cheer, ragged at first but growing to a solid roar, hit him. He clamped the door and locked it, then turned. "Places, men."

Art and Ross trotted to their hammocks, directly behind the pilots' seats. These hammocks were vertical, more like stretchers braced upright than garden hammocks. They snapped safety belts across their knees and chests.

Morrie was already in his chair, legs braced, safety belts buckled, head back against the shock pad. Cargraves slipped into the seat beside him, favoring his bad foot as he did so. "All set, Morrie." His eyes glanced over the instrument board, particularly noticing the temperature of the zinc and the telltale for position of the cadmium damping plates.

He buckled himself in and glanced out the quartz glass screen ahead of him. The field was clear as far as he could see. Staring straight at him, round and beautiful, was their destination. Under his right hand, mounted on the arm rest, was a large knurled knob. He grasped it.

"Art?"

"Ready, sir."

"Ross?"

"Ready, Captain."

"Co-pilot?"

"Ready, Captain. Time, six-oh-one."

He twisted the knob slowly to the right. Back behind him, actuated by remote control, cadmium shields slowly withdrew from between lattices of graphite and thorium; uncountable millions of neutrons found it easier to seek atoms of thorium to destroy. The tortured nuclei, giving up the ghost, spent their energy in boiling the molten zinc.

The ship began to tremble.

With his left hand he cut in the nose rockets, balancing them against the increasing surge from the rear. He slapped in the belly jets; the ship reared. He let the nose jets die.

The *Galileo* leaped forward, pressing them back into their pads.

They were headed skyward, out and far.

IX   INTO THE LONELY DEPTHS

To Ross and Art the world seemed to rotate dizzily through ninety degrees. They had been standing up, strapped to their upright hammocks, and staring straight forward past Cargraves and Morrie out through the conning port at the moon and the western horizon.

When the rocket took off it was as if they had been suddenly forced backwards, flat on their backs and pushed heavily into the cushions and springs. Which, in a way, was exactly what had happened to them. It was the powerful thrust of the jet which had forced them back against the springs and held them there. The force of the drive made the direction they were traveling "up."

But the moon still stared back at them, dead ahead through the port; "up" was also "west." From where they lay, flat on their backs, Cargraves and Morrie were above them and were kept from falling on them by the heavy steel thrust members which supported the piloting chairs.

The moon shimmered and boiled under the compression waves of air. The scream of the frantic molecules of air against the skin of the craft was louder and even more nerve-racking than steady thunder of the jet below them. The horizon dropped steadily away from the disk of the moon as they shot west and gained altitude. The sky, early morning gray as they took off, turned noonday blue as their flat climb took them higher and higher into the sunlight.

The sky started to turn purple and the stars came out. The scream of the air was less troublesome. Cargraves cut in his gyros and let Joe the Robot correct his initial course; the moon swung gently to the right about half its width and steadied. "Everybody all right?" he called out, his attention free of the controls for a moment.

"Swell!" Art called back.

"Somebody's sitting on my chest," Ross added.

"What's that?"

"I say, somebody's sitting on my chest!" Ross shouted.

"Well, wait a bit. His brother will be along in a minute."

"What did you say?"

"*Never mind!*" Cargraves shouted. "It wasn't important. Co-pilot!"

"Yes, Captain!"

"I'm going into full automatic. Get ready to check our course."

"Aye, aye, sir." Morrie clamped his octant near his face and shifted his head a little so that he could see the scope of the belly radar easily. He dug his head into the pads and braced his arms and hands; he knew what was coming. "Astrogator ready!"

The sky was black now and the stars were sharp. The image of the moon had ceased to shake and the unearthly scream of the air had died away, leaving only the tireless thunder of the jet. They were above the atmosphere, high and free.

Cargraves yelled, "Hang on to your hats, boys! *Here we go!*" He turned full control over to Joe the robot pilot. That mindless, mechanical-and-electronic worthy figuratively shook his non-existent head and decided he did not like the course. The image of the moon swung "down" and toward the bow, in terms of the ordinary directions in the ship, until the rocket was headed in a direction nearly forty degrees further east than was the image of the moon.

Having turned the ship to head for the point where the moon would be when the *Galileo* met it, rather than headed for where it now was, Joe turned his attention to the jet. The cadmium plates were withdrawn a little farther; the rocket really bit in and began to dig.

Ross found that there was indeed a whole family on his chest. Breathing was hard work and his eyes seemed foggy.

If Joe had had feelings he need have felt no pride in what he had just done, for his decisions had all been made for him before the ship left the ground. Morrie had selected, with Cargraves' approval, one of several three-dimensional cams and had installed it in Joe's innards. The cam "told" Joe what sort of a course to follow to the moon, what course to head first, how fast to gun the rocket and how long to keep it up. Joe could not see the moon—Joe had never heard of the moon—but his electronic senses could perceive how the ship was headed in relation to the steady, unswerving spin of the gyroes and then head the ship in the direction called for by the cam in his tummy.

The cam itself had been designed by a remote cousin of Joe's, the great "Eniac" computer at the University of Pennsylvania. By means of the small astrogation computer in the ship either Morrie or Cargraves could work out any necessary problem and control the *Galileo* by hand, but Joe, with the aid of his cousin, could do the same thing better, faster, more accurately and with unsleeping care—provided the human pilot knew what to ask of him and how to ask it.

Joe had not been invented by Cargraves; thousands of scientists, engineers, and mathematicians had contributed to his existence. His grandfathers had guided the Nazi V-2 rockets in the horror-haunted last days of World War II. His fathers had been developed for the deadly, ocean-spanning guided-missiles of the UN world police force. His brothers and sisters were found in every rocket ship, private and commercial, passenger-carrying or unmanned, that cleft the skies of earth.

Trans-Atlantic hop or trip to the moon, it was all one to Joe. He did what his cam told him to do. He did not care, he did not even know.

Cargraves called out," How you making out down there?"

"All right, I guess," Ross answered, his voice laboring painfully.

"I feel sick," Art admitted with a groan.

"Breathe through your mouth. Take deep breaths."

"I can't."

"Well, hang on. It won't be long."

In fact it was only fifty-five seconds at full drive until

Joe, still advised by his cam, decided that they had had enough of full drive. The cadmium plates slid father back into the power pile, thwarting the neutrons; the roar of the rocket drive lessened.

The ship did not slow down; it simply ceased to accelerate so rapidly. It maintained all the speed it had gained and the frictionless vaccum of space did nothing to slow its headlong plunge. But the acceleration was reduced to one earth-surface gravity, one g, enough to overcome the powerful tug of the earth's mighty weight and thereby permit the ship to speed ahead unchecked—a little less than one g, in fact, as the grasp of the earth was already loosening and would continue to drop off to the change-over, more than 200,000 miles out in space, where the attraction of the moon and that of the earth are equal.

For the four in the ship the reduction in the force of the jet had returned them to a trifle less than normal weight, under an artificial gravity produced by the drive of the jet. This false "gravity" had nothing to do with the pull of the earth; the attraction of the earth can be felt only when one is anchored to it and supported by it, its oceans, or its air.

The attraction of the earth exists out in space but the human body has no senses which can perceive it. If a man were to fall from a tremendous height, say fifty thousand miles, it would not seem to him that he was falling but rather that the earth was rushing up to meet him.

After the tremendous initial drive had eased off, Cargraves called out again to Art. "Feeling any better, kid?"

"I'm all right now," Art replied.

"Fine. Want to come up here where you can see better?"

"Sure!" responded both Art and Ross, with one voice.

"Okay. Watch your step."

"We will." The two unstrapped themselves and climbed up to the control station by means of hand and toe holds welded to the sides of the ship. Once there they squatted on the supporting beams for the pilots' chairs, one on each side. They looked out.

The moon had not been visible to them from their hammock positions after the change in course. From their new positions they could see it, near the "lower" edge of the conning port. It was full, silver white and so dazzling bright that it hurt their eyes, although not sufficiently nearer to produce any apparent increase in size. The stars around it in the coal-black sky were hard bright diamonds, untwinkling.

"Look at that," breathed Ross. "Look at old Tycho shining out like a searchlight. Boy!"

"I wish we could see the earth," said Art. "This bucket ought to have more than one view port."

"What do you expect for a dollar-six-bits?" asked Ross. "Chimes? The *Galileo* was a freighter."

"I can show it to you in the scope," Morrie offered, and switched on the piloting radar in the belly. The screen lit up after a few seconds but the picture was disappointing. Art could read it well enough—it was his baby—but esthetically it was unsatisfying. It was no more than a circular plot reading in bearing and distance; the earth was simply a vague mass of light on that edge of the circle which represented the astern direction.

"That's not what I want," Art objected. "I want to *see* it. I want to see it shape up like a globe and see the continents and the oceans."

"You'll have to wait until tomorrow, then, when we cut the drive and swing ship. Then you can see the earth and the sun, too."

"Okay. How fast are we going? Never mind—I see," he went on, peering at the instrument board. "3300 miles per hour."

"You're looking at it wrong," Ross corrected him. "It says 14,400 miles per hour."

"You're crazy."

"Like fun. Your eyes have gone bad."

"Easy, boys, easy," Cargraves counseled. "You are looking at different instruments. What kind of speed do you want?"

"I want to know how fast we're going," Art persisted.

"Now, Art, I'm surprised at you. After all, you've had every one of these instruments apart. Think what you're saying."

Art stared at the instrument board again, then looked sheepish. "Sure, I forgot. Let's see now—we've gained 14,000 and some, close to 15,000 now, miles per hour in free fall—but we're not falling."

"We're always falling," Morrie put in, smug for the moment in his status as pilot. "You fall all the time from the second you take off, but you drive to beat the fall."

"Yes, yes, I know," Art cut him off. "I was just mixed up for a moment. Thirty-three hundred is the speed I want—3310 now."

"Speed" in space is a curiously slippery term, as it is relative to whatever point you select as "fixed"—but the points in space are never fixed. The speed Art settled for was the speed of the *Galileo* along a line from the earth to their meeting place with the moon. This speed was arrived at deep inside Joe the Robot by combining by automatic vector addition three very complicated figures: first was the accumulated acceleration put on the ship by its jet drive, second the motions imposed on the ship by its closeness to the earth—its "free fall" speed of which Art had spoken. And lastly, there was the spin of the earth itself, considered both in amount and direction for the time of day of the take-off and the latitude of the camp site in New Mexico. The last was subtracted, rather than added, insofar as the terms of ordinary arithmetic apply to this sort of figuring.

The problem could be made vastly more complicated. The *Galileo* was riding with the earth and the moon in their yearly journey around the sun—at a speed of about 19 miles per second or approximately 70,000 miles per hour as seen from outer space. In addition, the earth-moon line was sweeping around the earth once each month as it followed the moon—but Joe the Robot had compensated for that when he set them on a course to where the moon *would be* rather than where it *was*.

There were also the complicated motions of the sun and

its planets with reference to the giddily whirling "fixed" stars, speeds which could be nearly anything you wanted, depending on which types of stars you selected for your reference points, but all of which speeds are measured in many miles per second.

But Joe cared nothing for these matters. His cam and his many circuits told him how to get them from the earth to the moon; he knew how to do that and Doctor Einstein's notions of relativity worried him not. The mass of machinery and wiring which made up his being did not have worry built into it. It was, however, capable of combining the data that came to it to show that the *Galileo* was now moving somewhat more than 3300 miles per hour along an imaginary line which joined earth to the point where the moon would be when they arrived.

Morrie could check this figure by radar observations for distance, plus a little arithmetic. If the positions as observed did not match what Joe computed them to be, Morrie could feed Joe the corrections and Joe would accept them and work them into his future calculations as placidly and as automatically as a well-behaved stomach changes starch into sugar.

"Thirty-three hundred miles per hour," said Art. "That's not so much. The V-2 rockets in the war made more than that. Let's open her up wide and see what she'll do. How about it, Doc?"

"Sure," agreed Ross, "we've got a clear road and plenty of room. Let's bust some space."

Cargraves sighed. "See here," he answered, "I did not try to keep you darned young speed demons from risking your necks in that pile of bailing wire you call an automobile, even when I jeopardized my own life by keeping quiet. But I'm going to run this rocket my way. I'm in no hurry."

"Okay, okay, just a suggestion," Ross assured him. He was quiet for a moment, then added, "But there's one thing that bothers me——"

"What?"

"Well, if I've read it once I've read it a thousand times,

that you have to go seven miles per second to get away from the earth. Yet here we are going only 3300 miles per hour."

"We're moving, aren't we?"

"Yeah, but——"

"As a matter of fact we are going to build up a lot more speed before we start to coast. We'll make the first part of the trip much faster than the last part. But suppose we just held our present speed—how long would it take to get to the moon?"

Ross did a little fast mental arithmetic concerning the distance of the moon from the earth, rounding the figure off to 240,000 miles. "About three days."

"What's wrong with that? Never mind," Cargraves went on. "I'm not trying to be a smart Aleck. The misconception is one of the oldest in the book, and it keeps showing up again, every time some non-technical man decides to do a feature story on the future of space travel. It comes from mixing up *shooting* with *rocketry*. If you wanted to fire a shot at the moon, the way Jules Verne proposed, it would have to go seven miles per second when it left the gun or it would fall back. But with a rocket you could make the crossing at a slow walk if you had enough power and enough fuel to keep on driving just hard enough to keep from falling back. Of course it would raise Cain with your mass-ratio. But we're doing something of that sort right now. We've got power to spare; I don't see why we should knock ourselves out with higher acceleration than we have to just to get there a little sooner. The moon will wait. It's waited a long time.

"Anyhow," he added, "no matter what you say and no matter how many physics textbooks are written and studied, people still keep mixing up gunnery and rocketry. It reminds me of that other old chestnut—about how a rocket can't work out in empty space, because it wouldn't have anything to *push* on.

"Go ahead and laugh!" Cargraves continued, seeing their expressions. "It strikes you as funny as a The-World-Is-Flat theory. But I heard an aeronautical engineer, as late as 1943, say just that."

"No! Not really!"

"I certainly did. He was a man with twenty-five years of professional experience and he had worked for both Wright Field and the Navy. But he said that in *1943*. Next year the Nazis were bombing London with V-2s. Yet according to him it couldn't be done!"

"I'd think any man who had ever felt the kick of a shotgun would understand how a rocket works," Ross commented.

"It doesn't work out that way. Mostly it has no effect on his brain cells; it just gives him a sore shoulder." He started to lift himself out of his semi-reclining position in his pilot's chair. "Come on. Let's eat. Wow! My foot's gone to sleep. I want to stoke up and then get some sleep. Breakfast wasn't much good for me—too many people staring down our necks."

"Sleep?" said Art. "Did you say 'sleep'? I can't sleep; I'm too excited. I don't suppose I'll sleep the whole trip."

"Suit yourself. Me, I'm going to soak up shut-eye just as soon as we've eaten. There's nothing to see now, and won't be until we go into free fall. You've had better views of the moon through the telescope."

"It's not the same thing," Art pointed out.

"No, it's not," Cargraves conceded. "Just the same, I intend to reach the moon rested up instead of worn out. Morrie, where did you stow the can openers?"

"I—" Morrie stopped and a look of utter consternation came over his face. "I think I left them behind. I put them down on the sink shelf and then some female reporter started asking me some fool question and——"

"Yeah, I saw," Ross interrupted him. "You were practically rolling over and playing dead for her. It was cute."

Cargraves whistled tunelessly. "I hope that we find out that we haven't left behind anything really indispensable. Never mind the can openers, Morrie. The way I feel I could open a can with my bare teeth."

"Oh, you won't have to do that, Doc," Morrie said eagerly.

"I've got a knife with a gadget for—" He was feeling in his pocket as he talked. His expression changed abruptly and he withdrew his hand. "Here are the can openers, Doc."

Ross looked at him innocently. "Did you get her address, Morrie?"

Supper, or late breakfast, as the case may be, was a simple meal, eaten from ration cans. Thereafter Cargraves got out his bedding roll and spread it on the bulkhead—now a deck—which separated the pilot compartment from the hold. Morrie decided to sleep in his co-pilot's chair. It, with its arm rests, head support, and foot rest, was not unlike an extremely well-padded barber's chair for the purpose, one which had been opened to a semi-reclining position. Cargraves let him try it, cautioning him only to lock his controls before going to sleep.

About an hour later Morrie climbed down and spread his roll beside Cargraves. Art and Ross slept on their acceleration hammocks, which were very well adapted to the purpose, as long as the occupant was not strapped down.

Despite the muted roar of the jet, despite the excitement of being in space, they all were asleep in a few minutes. They were dead tired and needed it.

During the "night" Joe the Robot slowly reduced the drive of the jet as the pull of the earth grew less.

Art was first to awaken. He had trouble finding himself for a moment or two and almost fell from his hammock on to the two sleepers below before he recollected his surroundings. When he did it brought him wide awake with a start. Space! He was out in space!—headed for the moon!

Moving with unnecessary quiet, since he could hardly have been heard above the noise of the jet in any case and since both Ross and Cargraves were giving very fair imitations of rocket motors themselves, he climbed out of the hammock and monkey-footed up to the pilots' seats. He dropped into Morrie's chair, feeling curiously but pleasantly light under the much reduced acceleration.

The moon, now visibly larger and almost painfully beautiful, hung in the same position in the sky, such that he had to let his gaze drop as he lay in the chair in order to return its stare. This bothered him for a moment—how were they ever to reach the moon if the moon did not draw toward the point where they were aiming?

It would not have bothered Morrie, trained as he was in a pilot's knowledge of collision bearings, interception courses, and the like. But, since it appeared to run contrary to common sense, Art worried about it until he managed to visualize the situation somewhat thus: if a car is speeding for a railroad crossing and a train is approaching from the left, so that their combined speeds will bring about a wreck, then the bearing of the locomotive from the automobile will not change, right up to the moment of the collision.

It was a simple matter of similar triangles, easy to see with a diagram but hard to keep straight in the head. The moon was speeding to their meeting place at about 2000 miles an hour, yet she would never change direction; she would simply grow and grow and grow until she filled the whole sky.

He let his eyes rove over her, naming the lovely names in his mind, Mare Tranquilitatis, Oceanus Procellarum, the lunar Apennines, LaGrange, Ptolemaeus, Mare Imbrium, Catharina. Beautiful words, they rolled on the tongue.

He was not too sure of the capitals of all the fifty-one United States and even naming the United Nations might throw him, but the geography—or was it lunography?—of the moon was as familiar to him as the streets of his home town.

This face of the moon, anyway—he wondered what the other face was like, the face the earth has never seen.

The dazzle of the moon was beginning to hurt his eyes; he looked up and rested them on the deep, black velvet of space, blacker by contrast with the sprinkle of stars.

There were few of the really bright stars in the region toward which the *Galileo* was heading. Aldebaran blazed forth, high and aft, across the port from the moon. The right-hand frame of the port slashed through the Milky Way and a small portion of that incredible river of stars was thereby left visible to him. He picked out the modest lights of Aries, and near mighty Aldebaran hung the ghostly, fairy Pleiades, but dead ahead, straight up, were only faint stars and a black and lonely waste.

He lay back, staring into this remote and solitary depth, vast and remote beyond human comprehension, until he was fascinated by it, drawn into it. He seemed to have left the warmth and safety of the ship and to be plunging deep into the silent blackness ahead.

He blinked his eyes and shivered, and for the first time felt himself wishing that he had never left the safe and customary and friendly scenes of home. He wanted his basement lab, his mother's little shop, and the humdrum talk of ordinary people, people who stayed home and did not worry about the outer universe.

Still the black depths fascinated him. He fingered the drive control under his right hand. He had only to unlock it, twist it all the way to the right, and they would plunge ahead, nailed down by unthinkable acceleration, and speed on past the moon, too early for their date in space with her. On past the moon, away from the sun and the earth behind them, on and on and out and out, until the thorium burned itself cold or until the zinc had boiled away, but not to stop even then, but to continue forever into the weary years and the bottomless depths.

He blinked his eyes and then closed them tight, and gripped both arms of the chair.

X THE METHOD OF SCIENCE

"Are you asleep?" the voice in his ear made Art jump; he had still had his eyes closed—it startled him. But it was only Doc, climbing up behind him.

"Oh! Good morning, Doc. Gee, I'm glad to see you. This place was beginning to give me the jim-jams."

"Good morning to you, if it is morning. I suppose it is morning, somewhere." He glanced at his watch. "I'm not surprised that you got the willies, up here by yourself. How would you like to make this trip by yourself?"

"Not me."

"Not me, either. The moon will be just about as lonely but it will feel better to have some solid ground underfoot. But I don't suppose this trip will be really popular until the moon has some nice, noisy night clubs and a bowling alley or two." He settled himself down in his chair.

"That's not very likely, is it?"

"Why not? The moon is bound to be a tourists' stop some day—and have you ever noticed how, when tourists get somewhere new, the first thing they do is to look up the same kind of entertainments they could find just as easily at home?"

Art nodded wisely, while tucking the notion away in his mind. His own experience with tourists and travel was slight —until now! "Say, Uncle, do you suppose I could get a decent picture of the moon through the port?"

Cargraves squinted up at it. "Might. But why waste film? They get better pictures of it from the earth. Wait until we go into a free orbit and swing ship. Then you can get some really unique pics—the earth from space. Or wait until we swing around the moon."

"That's what I really want! Pictures of the other side of the moon."

"What's what I thought." Cargraves paused a moment and then added, "But how do you know you can get any?"

"But . . . Oh, I see what you mean. It'll be dark on that side."

"That's not exactly what I meant, although that figures in, too, since the moon will be only about three days past 'new moon,' 'new moon,' that is, for the other side. We'll try to time it to get all the pics you want on the trip back. But that isn't what I mean: How do you know there is any back side to the moon? You've never seen it. Neither has any one else, for that matter."

"But—there has to—I mean, you can see . . ."

"Did I hear you say there wasn't any other side to the moon, Doc?" It was Ross, whose head had suddenly appeared beside Cargraves.

"Good morning, Ross. No, I did not say there was no other side to the moon. I had asked Art to tell me what leads him to think there *is* one."

Ross smiled. "Don't let him pull your leg, Art. He's just trying to rib you."

Cargraves grinned wickedly. "Okay, Aristotle, you picked it. Suppose you try to prove to me that there is a far side to the moon."

"It stands to reason."

"What sort of reason? Have you ever been there? Ever seen it?"

"No, but——"

"Ever met anybody who's ever seen it? Ever read any accounts by anybody who claimed to have seen it?"

"No, I haven't, but I'm sure there is one."

"Why?"

"Because I can see the front of it."

"What does that prove? Isn't your experience, up to now, limited to things you've seen on earth? For that matter I can name a thing you've seen on earth that hasn't any back side."

"Huh? What sort of a thing? What are you guys talking about?" It was Morrie this time, climbing up on the other side.

Art said, "Hi, Morrie. Want your seat?"

"No, thanks. I'll just squat here for the time being." He settled himself, feet dangling. "What's the argument?"

"Doc," Ross answered, "is trying to prove there isn't any other side to the moon."

"No, no, no," Cargraves hastily denied. "And repeat 'no.' I was trying to get you to prove your assertion that there was one. I was saying that there was a phenomenon even on earth which hasn't any back side, to nail down Ross's argument from experience with other matters—even allowing that earth experience necessarily applies to the moon, which I don't."

"Woops! Slow up! Take the last one first. Don't natural laws apply anywhere in the universe?"

"Pure assumption, unproved."

"But astronomers make predictions, eclipses and such, based on that assumption—and they work out."

"You've got it backwards. The Chinese were predicting eclipses long before the theory of the invariability of natural law was popular. Anyhow, at the best, we notice certain limited similarities between events in the sky and events on earth. Which has nothing to do with the question of a back side of the moon which we've never seen and may not be there."

"But we've seen a lot of it," Morrie pointed out.

"I get you," Cargraves agreed. "Between librations and such—the eccentricity of the moon's orbit and its tilt, we get to peek a little way around the edges from time to time and see about 60 per cent of its surface—*if* the surface is globular. But I'm talking about that missing 40 per cent that we've never seen."

"Oh," said Ross, "you mean the side we can't see might just be sliced off, like an apple with a piece out of it. Well, you may be right, but I'll bet you six chocolate malts, payable when we get back, that you're all wet."

"Nope," Cargraves answered, "this is a scientific discussion and betting is inappropriate. Besides, I might lose. But I did not mean anything of the slice-out-of-an-apple sort. I meant just what I said: no back side at all. The possibility that when we swing around the moon to look at the other side, we won't find anything at all, nothing, just empty space—that when we try to look at the moon from behind it, there won't be any moon to be seen—not from that position. I'm not asserting that that is what we will find; I'm asking you to *prove* that we will find anything."

"Wait a minute," Morrie put in, as Art glanced wildly at the moon as if to assure himself that it was still there—it was! "You mèntioned something of that sort on earth—a thing with no back. What was it? I'm from Missouri."

"A rainbow. You can see it from just one side, the side that faces the sun. The other side does not exist."

"But you can't get behind it."

"Then try it with a garden spray some sunny day. Walk around it. When you get behind it, it ain't there."

"Yes, but Doc," Ross objected, "you're just quibbling. The cases aren't parallel. A rainbow is just light waves; the moon is something substantial."

"That's what I'm trying to get you to prove, and you haven't proved it yet. How do you know the moon is substantial? All you have ever seen of it is just light waves, as with the rainbow."

Ross thought about this. "Okay, I guess I see what you're getting at. But we *do* know that the moon is substantial; they bounced radar off it, as far back as '46."

"Just light waves again, Ross. Infra-red light, or ultra-shortwave radio, but the same spectrum. Come again."

"Yes, but they *bounced*."

"You are drawing an analogy from earth conditions again. I repeat, we know nothing of moon conditions except through the insubstantial waves of the electromagnetic spectrum."

"How about tides?"

"Tides exist, certainly. We have seen them, wet our feet in them. But that proves nothing about the moon. The theory that the moon causes the tides is a sheer convenience, pure theory. We change theories as often as we change our underwear. Next year it may be simpler to assume that the tides cause the moon. Got any other ideas?"

Ross took a deep breath. "You're trying to beat me down with words. All right, so I haven't seen the other side of the moon. So I've never felt the moon, or taken a bite out of it. By the way, you can hang on to the theory that the moon is made of green cheese with that line of argument."

"Not quite," said Cargraves. "There is some data on that, for what it's worth. An astronomer fellow made a spectrograph of green cheese and compared it with a spectrograph of the moon. No resemblance."

Art chortled. "He didn't, really?"

"Fact. You can look it up."

Ross shrugged. "That's no better than the radar data," he said correctly. "But to get on with my proof. Granted that there is a front side to the moon, whatever its nature, just as long as it isn't so insubstantial that it won't even reflect radar, then there has to be some sort of a back, flat, round, square, or wiggly. That's a matter of certain mathematical deduction."

Morrie snorted.

Cargraves limited himself to a slight smile. "Now, Ross. Think it over. What is the content of mathematics?"

"The content of mathe—" He collapsed suddenly. "Oh . . . I guess I finally get it. Mathematics doesn't have any content. If we found there wasn't any other side, then we would just have to invent a new mathematics."

"That's the idea. Fact of the matter is, we won't *know* that there is another side to the moon until we get there. I was just trying to show you," he went on, "just how insubstantial a 'common sense' idea can be when you pin it down. Neither 'common sense' nor 'logic' can *prove* anything. Proof comes from experiment, or to put it another way, from experience, and from nothing else. Short lecture on the scientific method—you can count it as thirty minutes on today's study time. Anybody else want breakfast but me? Or has the low weight made you queasy?" He started to climb out of his chair.

Ross was very thoughtful while they made preparations for breakfast. This was to be a proper meal, prepared from their limited supply of non-canned foods. The *Galileo* had been fitted with a galley of sorts, principally a hot plate and a small refrigerator. Dishes and knives, forks, and spoons could be washed, sparingly, with the water which accumulated in the sump of the air-conditioner, and then sterilized on the hot plate. The ship had everything necessary to life, even a cramped but indispensable washroom. But every auxiliary article, such as dishes, was made of zinc—reserve mass for the hungry jet.

They sat, or rather squatted, down to a meal of real milk, cereal, boiled eggs, rolls, jam, and coffee. Cargraves sighed contentedly when it had been tucked away. "We won't get many like that," he commented, as he filled his pipe. "Space travel isn't all it's cracked up to be, not yet."

"Mind the pipe, Skipper!" Morrie warned.

Cargraves looked startled. "I forgot," he admitted guiltily. He stared longingly at the pipe. "Say, Ross," he inquired, "do you think the air-conditioner would clean it out fast enough?"

"Go ahead. Try it," Ross urged him. "One pipeful won't kill us. But say, Doc——"

"Yes?"

"Well, uh, look—don't you really *believe* there is another side to the moon?"

"Huh? Still on that, eh? Of course I do."

"But——"

"But it's just my opinion. I believe it because all my assumptions, beliefs, prejudices, theories, superstitions, and so forth, tend that way. It's part of the pattern of fictions I live by, but that doesn't prove it's right. So if it turns out to be wrong I hope I am sufficiently emotionally braced not to blow my top.

"Which brings us right back to study time," he went on.

"You've all got thirty minutes' credit, which gives you an hour and a half to go. Better get busy."

Art looked dumfounded. "I thought you were kidding, Uncle. You don't mean to run such a schedule *on the moon*, do you?"

"Unless circumstances prevent. Now is a good time to work up a little reserve, for that matter, while there is nothing to see and no work to do."

Art continued to look astonished, then his face cleared. "I'm afraid we can't, Uncle. The books are all packed down so far that we can't get at them till we land."

"So? Well, we won't let that stop us. A school," he quoted, "is a log with a pupil on one end and a teacher on the other. We'll have lectures and quizzes—starting with a review quiz. Gather round, victims."

They did so, sitting cross-legged in a circle on the hold bulkhead. Cargraves produced a pencil and a reasonably clean piece of paper from his always bulging pockets. "You first, Art. Sketch and describe a cyclotron. Basic review—let's see how much you've forgotten."

Art commenced outlining painfully the essential parts of a cyclotron. He sketched two hollow half-cylinders, with their open sides facing each other, close together. "These are made of copper," he stated, "and each one is an electrode for a very high frequency, high voltage power source. It's actually a sort of short-wave radio transmitter—I'll leave it out of the sketch. Then you have an enormously powerful electromagnet with its field running through the opening between the dees, the half-cylinders, and vertical to them. The whole thing is inside a big vacuum chamber. You get a source of ions——"

"What sort of ions?"

"Well, maybe you put a little hydrogen in the vacuum chamber and kick it up with a hot filament at the center point of the two dees. Then you get hydrogen nuclei—protons."

"Go ahead."

"The protons have a positive charge, of course. The

alternating current would keep them kicking back and forth between the two electrodes—the dees. But the magnetic field, since the protons are charged particles, tends to make them whirl around in circles. Between the two of them, the protons go whirling around in a spiral, gaining speed each revolution until they finally fly out a little thin, metal window in the vacuum chamber, going to beat the band."

"But why bother?"

"Well, if you aim this stream of high-speed protons at some material, say a piece of metal, things begin to happen. It can knock electrons off the atoms, or it can even get inside and stir up the nuclei and cause transmutations or make the target radioactive—things like that."

"Good enough," Cargraves agreed, and went on to ask him several more questions to bring out details. "Just one thing," he said afterwards. "You know the answers, but just between ourselves, that sketch smells a bit. It's sloppy."

"I never did have any artistic talent," Art said defensively. "I'd rather take a photograph any day."

"You've taken too many photographs, maybe. As for artistic talent, I haven't any either, but I learned to sketch. Look, Art—the rest of you guys get this, too—if you can't sketch, you can't see. If you really see what you're looking at, you can put it down on paper, accurately. If you really remember what you have looked at, you can sketch it accurately from memory."

"But the lines don't go where I intend them to."

"A pencil will go where you push it. It hasn't any life of its own. The answer is practice and more practice and thinking about what you are looking at. All of you lugs want to be scientists. Well, the ability to sketch accurately is as necessary to a scientist as his slipstick. More necessary, you can get along without a slide rule. Okay, Art. You're next, Ross. Gimme a quick tell on the protactinium radioactive series."

Ross took a deep breath. "There are three families of radioactive isotopes: the uranium family, the thorium family, and the protoactinium family. The last one starts with isotope U-235 and—" They kept at it for considerably longer than an hour and a half, for Cargraves had the intention of letting them be as free as possible later, while still keeping to the letter and spirit of his contract with Ross's father.

At last he said, "I think we had better eat again. The drive will cut out before long. It's been cutting down all the time—notice how light you feel?"

"How about a K-ration?" inquired Morrie, in his second capacity as commissary steward.

"No, I don't think so," Cargraves answered slowly. "I think maybe we had better limit this meal to some amino acids and some gelatine." He raised his eyebrows.

"Umm—I see," Morrie agreed, glancing at the other two. "Maybe you are right." Morrie and Cargraves, being pilots, had experienced free fall in school. The stomachs of Ross and Art were still to be tried.

"What's the idea?" Art demanded.

Ross looked disgusted. "Oh, he thinks we'll toss our cookies. Why, we hardly weigh anything now. What do you take us for, Doc? Babies?"

"No," said Cargraves, "but I still think you might get dropsick. I did. I think predigested foods are a good idea."

"Oh, shucks. My stomach is strong. I've never been air sick."

"Ever been seasick?"

"I've never been to sea."

"Well, suit yourself," Cargraves told him. "But one thing I insist on. Wear a sack over your face. I don't want what you lose in the air-conditioner." He turned away and started preparing some gelatine for himself by simply pouring the powder into water, stirring, and drinking.

Ross made a face but he did not dig out a K-ration. Instead he switched on the hot plate, preparatory to heating milk for amino-acid concentrates.

A little later Joe the Robot awoke from his nap and switched off the jet completely.

They did not bounce up to the ceiling. The rocket did not spin wildly. None of the comic-strip things happened to them. They simply gradually ceased to weigh anything as the thrust died away. Almost as much they noticed the deafening new silence. Cargraves had previously made a personal inspection of the entire ship to be sure that everything was tied, clamped, or stored firmly so that the ship would not become cluttered up with loosely floating bric-a-brac.

Cargraves lifted himself away from his seat with one hand, turned in the air like a swimmer, and floated gently down, or rather across—up and down had ceased to exist—to where Ross and Art floated, loosely attached to their hammocks by a single belt as an added precaution. Cargraves checked his progress with one hand and steadied himself by grasping Art's hammock. "How's everybody?"

"All right, I guess," Art answered, gulping. "It feels like a falling elevator." He was slightly green.

"You, Ross?"

"I'll get by," Ross declared, and suddenly gagged. His color was gray rather than green.

Space sickness is not a joke, as every cadet rocket pilot knows. It is something like seasickness, like the terrible, wild retching that results from heavy pitching of a ship at sea—except that the sensation of everything dropping out from under one does not stop!

But the longest free-flight portions of a commercial rocket flight from point to point on earth last only a few minutes, with the balance of the trip on thrust or in glide, whereas the course Cargraves had decided on called for many hours of free fall. He could have chosen, with the power at his disposal, to make the whole trip on the jet, but that would have prevented them from turning ship, which he proposed to do now, until the time came to invert and drive the jet toward the moon to break their fall.

Only by turning the ship would they be able to see the earth from space; Cargraves wanted to do so before the earth was too far away.

"Just stay where you are for a while," he cautioned them. "I'm about to turn ship."

"I want to see it," Ross said stoutly. "I've been looking forward to it." He unbuckled his safety belt, then suddenly he was retching again. Saliva overflowed and drooled out curiously, not down his chin but in large droplets that seemed undecided where to go.

"Use your handkerchief," Cargraves advised him, feeling none too well himself. "Then come along if you feel like it." He turned to Art.

Art was already using his handkerchief.

Cargraves turned away and floated back to the pilot's chair. He was aware that there was nothing that he could do for them, and his own stomach was doing flip-flops and slow, banked turns. He wanted to strap his safety belt across it. Back in his seat, he noticed that Morrie was doubled up and holding his stomach, but he said nothing and gave his attention to turning the ship. Morrie would be all right.

Swinging the ship around was a very simple matter. Located at the center of gravity of the ship was a small, heavy, metal wheel. He had controls on the panel in front of him whereby he could turn this wheel to any axis, as it was mounted freely on gymbals, and then lock the gymbals. An electric motor enabled him to spin it rapidly in either direction and to stop it afterwards.

This wheel by itself could turn the ship when it was in free fall and then hold it in the new position. (It must be clearly understood that this turning had no effect at all on the course or speed of the *Galileo*, but simply on its attitude, the direction it faced, just as a fancy diver may turn and twist in falling from a great height, without thereby disturbing his fall.)

The little wheel was able to turn the huge vessel by a very simple law of physics, but in an application not often seen on the earth. The principle was the conservation of momentum, in this case angular momentum or spin. Ice skaters understand the application of this law; some of their fanciest tricks depend on it.

As the little wheel spun rapidly in one direction the big ship spun slowly in the other direction. When the wheel stopped, the ship stopped and just as abruptly.

"Dark glasses, boys!" Cargraves called out belatedly as the ship started to nose over and the stars wheeled past the port. In spite of their wretched nausea they managed to find their goggles, carried on their persons for this event, and get them on.

They needed them very soon. The moon slid away out of sight. The sun and the earth came into view. The earth was a great shining crescent like a moon two days past new. At this distance—one-fourth the way to the moon—it appeared sixteen times as wide as the moon does from the earth and many times more magnificent. The horns of the crescent were blue-white from the polar ice caps. Along its length showed the greenish blue of sea and the deep greens and sandy browns of ocean and forest and field . . . for the line of light and dark ran through the heart of Asia and down as if it had been a globe standing across a school room from them. The Indian Ocean was partly obscured by a great cloud bank, stormy to those underneath it perhaps, but blazing white as the polar caps to those who watched from space.

In the arms of the crescent was the nightside of earth, lighted dimly but plainly by the almost full moon behind them. But—and this is never seen on the moon when "the new moon holds the old moon in her arms"—the faintly lighted dark face was picked out here and there with little jewels of light, the cities of earth, warm and friendly and beckoning!

Halfway from equator to northern horn were three bright ones, not far apart—London, and Paris, and reborn Berlin. Across the dark Atlantic, at the very edge of the disk, was one especially bright and rosy light, the lights of Broadway and all of Greater New York.

All three of the boys were seeing New York for the first time, not to mention most of the rest of the great globe!

But, although it was their home, although they were

seeing it from a glorious vantage point new to mankind, their attention was torn away from the earth almost at once. There was a still more breath-taking object in the sky—the sun.

Its apparent width was only one-sixteenth that of the mighty crescent earth, but it brooked no competition. It hung below the earth—below when referred to the attitude of the *Galileo,* not in the sense of "up" or "down"—and about four times the width of the earth away. It was neither larger nor smaller than it appears from the earth and not appreciably brighter than it is on a clear, dry desert noon. But the sky was black around it in the airless space; its royal corona shone out; its prominences could be seen; its great infernal storms showed on its face.

"Don't look too directly at it," Cargraves warned, "even when you have the polarizer turned to maximum interference." He referred to the double lenses the boys wore, polaroid glass with the outer lens rotatable.

"I gotta have a picture of this!" Art declared, and turned and swam away. He had forgotten that he was space sick.

He was back shortly with his Contax and was busy fitting his longest lens into it. The camera was quite old, being one of the few things his mother had managed to bring out of Germany, and was his proudest possession. The lens in place, he started to take his Weston from its case. Cargraves stopped him.

"Why burn out your light meter?" he cautioned.

Art stopped suddenly. "Yes, I guess I would," he admitted. "But how am I going to get a picture?"

"Maybe you won't. Better use your slowest film, your strongest filter, your smallest stop, and your shortest exposure. Then pray."

Seeing that the boy looked disappointed, he went on, "I wouldn't worry too much about pictures of the sun. We can leave that to the astronomers who will follow us after we've blazed the trail. But you ought to be able to get a swell picture of the earth. Waste a little film on the sun first, then we will try it. I'll shade your lens from the sunlight with my hand."

Art did so, then prepared to photograph the earth. "I can't get a decent light reading on it, either," he complained. "Too much interference from the sun."

"Well, you *know* how much light it is getting—the works. Why not assume it's about like desert sunlight, then shoot a few both above and below what that calls for?"

When Art had finished Cargraves said, "Mind the sunburn, boys." He touched the plastic inner layer of the quartz port. "This stuff is supposed to filter out the worst of it—but take it easy."

"Shucks, we're tanned." And so they were; New Mexico sun had left its mark.

"I know, but that's the brightest sunshine you ever saw. Take it easy."

"How much chance is there," asked Morrie, "that this pure stuff is dangerous? I mean aside from bad sunburn."

"You read the same papers I did. We're getting more cosmic radiation, too. Maybe it'll knock us down dead. Maybe it'll cause your children to have long green tendrils. That's one of the chances we take."

"Well, Columbus took a chance."

"And look how far he got!" put in Art.

"Yeah, thrown in the hoosegow for his trouble."

"Be that as it may," said Cargraves, "I'm going to turn the ship again so that the sun doesn't shine in so directly. This tub is getting too hot." It was no trouble to keep the *Galileo* warm enough, but how to get rid of unwanted heat was another matter. Her polished sides reflected most of the heat that struck them, but sunshine pouring directly in the view port produced a most uncomfortable greenhouse effect. Refrigeration, in the ordinary sense, was no answer; the ship was a closed system and could lose heat only by radiation to outer space. At the moment she was absorbing radiant heat from the sun much faster than she was radiating it.

"I want to take some more pictures," Art protested.

"I'll keep the earth in sight," Cargraves promised, and set the controls of the spinning wheel to suit his purpose. Then he floated back to the view port and joined the others, who were swimming in front of it like goldfish in a bowl.

Ross touched the transparent wall with a finger tip; the light contact pushed him back from the port. "Doc, what do you think would happen if a meteor hit this port?"

"I don't like to think about it. However, I wouldn't worry too much about it. Ley has calculated that the chance of being hit by a meteor on a trip out to the moon and back is about one in a half a million. I figure I was in much graver danger every time I climbed into that alleged autombile you guys drive."

"That's a good car."

"I'll admit it performs well." He turned away with a motion much like that of a sprint swimmer turning on the side of a pool. "Art, when you are through snapping that Brownie, I've got something better for you to do. How about trying to raise earth?"

"Just one more of— Huh? What did you say?"

"How about heating up your tubes and seeing if there is anybody on the air—or lack-of-air, as the case may be?"

No attempt had been made to use the radios since blasting off. Not only did the jet interfere seriously, but also the antennae were completely retracted, even spike antennae, during the passage through the atmosphere. But now that the jet was silent an attempt at communication seemed in order.

True, the piloting radar had kept them in touch by radio, in a manner of speaking, during the early part of the journey, but they were now beyond the range of the type of equipment used for piloting. It bore little resemblance to the giant radars used to bounce signals against the moon. The quartz windows through which it operated would have been quite inadequate for the large antenna used to fling power from the earth to the moon.

Art got busy at once, while stating that he thought the chances of picking up anything were slim. "It would have to be beamed tight as a, as a, well—tight. And why would anybody be beaming stuff out this way?"

"At us, of course," Ross offered.

"They can't find us. Radar won't pick up anything as small as this ship at this distance—too little mirror cross section." Art spoke authoritatively. "Not the radars they've got so far. Maybe some day, if—hey!"

"What have you got?"

"Keep quiet!" Art stared ahead with that look of painful, unseeing concentration found only under a pair of earphones. He twiddled his dials carefully, then fumbled for pencil and paper. Writing, he found, was difficult without gravity to steady himself and his hand. But he scribbled.

"Get a load of this," he whispered a few minutes later. He read:

"RADIO PARIS CALLING ROCKET SHIP *GALILEO* RADIO PARIS CALLING ROCKET SHIP *GALILEO* RADIO PARIS CALLING ROCKET SHIP *GALILEO* DOCTOR DONALD CARGRAVES ARTHUR MUELLER MAURICE ABRAMS ROSS JENKINS GREETINGS YOUR FLIGHT FOLLOWED UNTIL OH ONE ONE THREE GREENWICH TIME SEPTEMBER TWENTY FIFTH CONTACT LOST WILL CONTINUE TO CALL YOU ON THIS BEAM AND FREQUENCY FOLLOWING PROBABLE TRAJECTORY GOOD LUCK TO YOU RADIO PARIS CALLING ROCKET SHIP *GALILEO* RADIO PARIS——

"And then they repeat. It's a recording." His voice was shaky.

"Gosh!" Ross had no other comment.

"Well, boys, it looks like we're celebrities." Cargraves tried to make his words sound casual. Then he found that he was holding a piece of his pipe in each hand; he had broken it in two without knowing it. Shrugging, he let the piece float away from him.

"But how did they find us?" persisted Art.

"The message shows it," Morrie pointed out. "See that time? That's the time we went into free fall. They followed the jet."

"How? By telescope?"

"More likely," Cargraves put in, "by anti-rocket radiation tracer."

"Huh? But the UN patrol are the only ones with that sort of gear."

Cargraves permitted himself a grin. "And why shouldn't the UN be interested in us? See here, kid—can you squirt anything back at them?"

"I'll sure try!"

XI   ONE ATOM WAR TOO MANY?

ART GOT BUSY AT HIS TASK, but nothing came back which would tell him whether or not his attempts had been successful. The recording continued to come in whenever he listened for it, between attempts to send, for the next three and a . half hours. Then it faded out—they were off the beam.

Nevertheless, it was the longest direct communication of record in human history.

The *Galileo* continued her climb up from earth, toward that invisible boundary where the earth ceased to claim title and the lesser mass of the moon took charge. Up and up, out and farther out, rising in free flight, slowing from the still effective tug of the earth but still carried on by the speed she had attained under the drive of the jet, until at last the *Galileo* slipped quietly over the border and was in the moon's back yard. From there on she accelerated slowly as she fell toward the silvery satellite.

They ate and slept and ate again. They stared at the receding earth. And they slept again.

While they slept, Joe the Robot stirred, consulted his cam, decided that he had had enough of this weightlessness, and started the jet. But first he straightened out the ship so that the jet faced toward the moon, breaking their fall, while the port stared back at earth.

The noise of the jet woke them up. Cargraves had had them strap themselves down in anticipation of weight. They unstrapped and climbed up to the control station. "Where's the moon?" demanded Art.

"Under us, of course," Morrie informed him.

"Better try for it with radar, Morrie," Cargraves directed.

"Check!" Morrie switched on the juice, waited for it to warm, then adjusted it. The moon showed as a large vague mass on one side of the scope. "About fifteen thousand miles," he declared. "We'd better do some checking, Skipper."

They were busy for more than an hour, taking sights, taking readings, and computing. The bearing and distance of the moon, in relation to the ship, were available by radar. Direct star sights out the port established the direction of drive of the ship. Successive radar readings established the course and speed of the ship for comparison with the courses and speeds as given by the automatic instruments showing on the board. All these factors had to be taken into consideration in computing a check on the management of Joe the Robot.

Minor errors were found and the corrections were fed to the automatic pilot. Joe accepted the changes in his orders without comment.

While Morrie and Cargraves did this, Art and Ross were preparing the best meal they could throw together. It was a relief to have weight under their feet and it was a decided relief to their stomachs. Those organs had become adjusted to free fall, but hardly reconciled. Back on firm footing they hollered for solid food.

The meal was over and Cargraves was thinking sadly of his ruined pipe, when the control alarm sounded. Joe the Robot had completed his orders, his cam had run out, he called for relief.

They all scrambled up to the control station. The moon, blindingly white and incredibly huge was shouldering its way into one side of the port. They were so close to it now that their progress was visible, if one looked closely, by sighting across the frame of the port at some fixed object, a crater or a mountain range.

"Whee!" Art yelled.

"Kinda knocks your eyes out, doesn't it?" Ross said, gazing in open wonder.

"It does," agreed Cargraves. "But we've got work to do. Get back and strap yourself down and stand by for maneuvering."

While he complied, he strapped himself into his chair and then flipped a switch which ordered Joe to go to sleep; he was in direct, manual command of the rocket. With Morrie to coach him by instrument, he put the ship through a jockeying series of changes, gentle on the whole and involving only minor changes in course at any one time, but all intended to bring the ship from the flat conoid trajectory it had been following into a circular orbit around the moon.

"How'm I doin'?" he demanded a long time later.

"Right in the groove," Morrie assured him, after a short delay.

"Sure enough of it for me to go automatic and swing ship?"

"Let me track her a few more minutes." Presently Morrie assured him as requested. They had already gone into free flight just before Cargraves asked for a check. He now called out to Art and Ross that they could unstrap. He then started the ship to swinging so that the port faced toward the moon and switched on a combination which told Joe that he must get back to work; it was now his business to watch the altitude by radar and to see to it that altitude and speed remained constant.

Art was up at the port, with his camera, by the time he and Morrie had unstrapped.

"Goshawmighty," exclaimed Art, "this is something!" He unlimbered his equipment and began snapping frantically, until Ross pointed out that his lens cover was still on. Then he steadied down.

Ross floated face down and stared out at the desolation. They were speeding silently along, only two hundred miles above the ground, and they were approaching the sunrise line of light and darkness. The shadows were long on the barren wastes below them, the mountain peaks and the great gaping craters more horrendous on that account. "It's scary," Ross decided. "I'm not sure I like it."

"Want off at the next corner?" Cargraves inquired.

"No, but I'm not dead certain I'm glad I came."

Morrie grasped his arm, to steady himself apparently, but quite as much for the comfort of solid human companionship. "You know what I think, Ross," he began, as he stared out at the endless miles of craters. "I think I know how it got that way. Those aren't volcanic craters, that's certain—and it wasn't done by meteors. *They did it themselves!*"

"Huh? Who?"

"The moon people. They did it. They wrecked themselves. They ruined themselves. *They had one atomic war too many.*"

"Huh? What the—" Ross stared, then looked back at the surface as if to read the grim mystery there. Art stopped taking pictures.

"How about it, Doc?"

Cargraves wrinkled his brow. "Could be," he admitted. "None of the other theories for natural causes hold water for one reason or another. It would account for the relatively smooth parts we call 'seas.' They really were seas; that's why they weren't hit very hard."

"And that's why they aren't seas any more," Morrie went on. "They blew their atmosphere off and the seas boiled away. Look at Tycho. That's where they set off the biggest ammunition dump on the planet. It cracked the whole planet. I'll bet somebody worked out a counter-weapon that worked too well. It set off every atom bomb on the moon all at once and it ruined them! I'm sure of it."

"Well," said Cargraves, "I'm not sure of it, but I admit the theory is attractive. Perhaps we'll find out when we land. The notion of setting off all the bombs at once—there are strong theoretical objections to that. Nobody has any idea how to do it."

"Nobody knew how to make an atom bomb a few years ago," Morrie pointed out.

"That's true." Cargraves wanted to change the subject; it was unpleasantly close to horrors that had haunted his dreams since the beginning of World War II. "Ross, how do you feel about the other side of the moon now?"

"We'll know pretty soon," Ross chuckled. "Say—this *is* the Other Side!"

And so it was. They had leveled off in their circular orbit near the left limb of the moon as seen from the earth and were coasting over the mysterious other face. Ross scanned it closely. "Looks about the same."

"Did you expect anything different?"

"No, I guess not. But I had hoped." Even as he spoke they crossed the sunrise line and the ground below them was dark, not invisible, for it was still illuminated by faint starlight—starlight only, for the earthshine never reached this face. The suncapped peaks receded rapidly in the distance. At the rate they were traveling, a speed of nearly 4000 miles per hour necessary to maintain them in a low-level circular orbit, the complete circuit of the planet would take a little over an hour and a half.

"No more pictures, I guess," Art said sadly. "I wish it was a different time of the month."

"Yes," agreed Ross, still peering out, "it's a dirty shame to be this close and not see anything."

"Don't be impatient," Cargraves told him; "when we start

back in eight or nine days, we swing around again and you can stare and take pictures till you're cross-eyed."

"Why only eight or nine days? We've got more food than that."

"Two reasons. The first is, if we take off at new moon we won't have to stare into the sun on the way back. The second is, I'm homesick and I haven't even landed yet." He grinned. In utter seriousness he felt that it was not wise to stretch their luck by sticking around too long.

The trip across the lighted and familiar face of the moon was delightful, but so short that it was like window shopping in a speeding car. The craters and the "seas" were old familiar friends, yet strange and new. It reminded them of the always strange experience of seeing a famous television star on a personal appearance tour—recognition with an odd feeling of unreality.

Art shifted over to the motion-picture camera once used to record the progress of the *Starstruck* series, and got a complete sequence from *Mare Fecunditatis* to the crater Kepler, at which point Cargraves ordered him emphatically to stop at once and strap himself down.

They were coming into their landing trajectory. Cargraves and Morrie had selected a flat, unnamed area beyond *Oceanus Procellarum* for the landing because it was just on the border between the earth side and the unknown side, and thereby fitted two plans: to attempt to establish radio contact with earth, for which direct line-of-sight would be necessary, and to permit them to explore at least a portion of the unknown side.

Joe the Robot was called again and told to consult a second cam concealed in his dark insides, a cam which provided for the necessary braking drive and the final ticklish contact on maneuvering jets and radar. Cargraves carefully leveled the ship at the exact altitude and speed Joe would need for the approach and slipped over to automatic when Morrie signaled that they were at the exact, precalculated distance necessary for the landing.

Joe took over. He flipped the ship over, using the maneuvering rockets, then started backing in to a landing, using the jet in the tail to kill their still tremendous speed. The moon was below them now and Cargraves could see nothing but the stars, the stars and the crescent of the earth—a quarter of a million miles away and no help to him now.

He wondered if he would ever set foot on it again.

Morrie was studying the approach in the radar scope. "Checking out to nine zeros, Captain," he announced proudly and with considerable exaggeration. "It's in the bag."

The ground came up rapidly in the scope. When they were close and no longer, for the moment, dropping at all, Joe cut the main jet and flipped them over.

When he had collected himself from the wild gyration of the somersault, Cargraves saw the nose jets reach out and splash in front of them and realized that the belly jets were in play, too, as the surge of power pushed the seat of the chair up against him. He felt almost as if he could land it himself, it seemed so much like his first wild landing on the New Mexico desert.

Then for one frantic second he saw the smooth, flat ground ahead of the splash of the plowing nose jets give way to a desolation of rocky ridges, sharp crevasses, loose and dangerous cosmic rubble . . . soil from which, if they landed without crashing, they could not hope to take off.

The sunlight had fooled them. With the sun behind them the badlands had cast no shadows they could see; the flat plain had appeared to stretch to the mountains ahead. These were no mountains, but they were quite sufficient to wreck the *Galileo*.

The horrible second it took him to size up the situation was followed by frantic action. With one hand he cut the automatic pilot; with the other he twisted violently on the knob controlling the tail jet. He slapped the belly jets on full.

Her nose lifted.

She hung there, ready to fall, kept steady on her jets only by her gyros. Then slowly, slowly, slowly, the mighty tail jet reached out—so slowly that he knew at that moment that the logy response of the atomic pile would never serve him for what he had to do next, which was to land her himself.

The *Galileo* pulled away from the surface of the moon. "That was close," Morrie said mildly.

Cargraves wiped the sweat from his eyes and shivered. He knew what was called for now, in all reason. He knew that he should turn the ship away from the moon, head her in the general direction of the earth and work out a return path, a path to a planet with an atmosphere to help a pilot put down his savage ship. He knew right then that he was not the stuff of heroes, that he was getting old and knew it.

But he hated to tell Morrie.

"Going to put her down on manual?" the boy inquired.

"Huh?"

"That's the only way we'll get her down on a strange field. I can see that now—you've got to be able to see your spot at the last half minute—nose jets and no radar."

"I can't do it, Morrie."

The younger man said nothing. He simply sat and stared ahead without expression.

"I'm going to head her back to earth, Morrie."

The boy gave absolutely no sign of having heard him. There was neither approval nor disapproval on his face, nor any faint suggestion.

Cargraves thought of the scene when Ross, blind and bandaged, had told him off. Of Art, quelling his space sickness to get his pictures. He thought, too, of the hot and tiring days when he and Morrie had qualified for piloting together.

The boy said nothing, neither did he look at him.

These kids, these damn kids! How had he gotten up here, with a rocket under his hand and a cargo of minors to be responsible for? He was a laboratory scientist, not a superman. If it had been Ross, if Ross were a pilot—even where he now was, he shivered at the recollection of Ross's hair-raising driving. Art was about as bad. Morrie was worse.

He knew he would never be a hot pilot—not by twenty

years. These kids, with their casual ignorance, with their hot rod rigs, it was for them; piloting was their kind of a job. They were too young and too ignorant to care and their reflexes were not hobbled by second thoughts. He remembered Ross's words: "I'll go to the moon if I have to walk!"

"Land her, Morrie."

"Aye, aye, sir!"

The boy never looked at him. He flipped her up on her tail, then let her drop slowly by easing off on the tail jet. Purely by the seat of his pants, by some inner calculation—for Cargraves could see nothing through the port but stars, and neither could the boy—he flipped her over again, cutting the tail jet as he did so.

The ground was close to them and coming up fast.

He kicked her once with the belly jets, placing them thereby over a smooth stretch of land, and started taking her down with quick blasts of the nose jets, while sneaking a look between blasts.

When he had her down so close that Cargraves was sure that he was going to land her on her nose, crushing in the port and killing them, he gave her one more blast which made her rise a trifle, kicked her level and brought her down on the belly jets, almost horizontal, and so close to the ground that Cargraves could see it ahead of them, out the port.

Glancing casually out the port, Morrie gave one last squirt with the belly jets and let her settle. They grated heavily and were stopped. The *Galileo* sat on the face of the moon.

"Landed, sir. Time: Oh-eight-three-four."

Cargraves drew in a breath. "A beautiful, beautiful landing, Morrie."

"Thanks, Captain."

XII "THE BARE BONES—"

Ross AND ART WERE ALREADY out of their straps and talking loudly about getting out the space suits when Cargraves climbed shakily out of his chair—and then nearly fell. The lowered gravitation, one-sixth earth-normal, fooled him. He was used to weightlessness by now, and to the chest-binding pressure of high acceleration; the pseudo-normal weight of a one-g drive was no trouble, and maneuvering while strapped down was no worse than stunting in an airplane.

This was different and required a little getting used to, he decided. It reminded him a little of walking on rubber, or the curiously light-footed feeling one got after removing snow shoes or heavy boots.

Morrie remained at his post for a few moments longer to complete and sign his log. He hesitated over the space in the log sheet marked "position." They had taught him in school to enter here the latitude and longitude of the port of arrival—but what were the latitude and longitude of this spot?

The moon had its north and south poles just as definitely as the earth, which gave any spot a definite latitude, nor was longitude uncertain once a zero meridian was selected. That had been done; Tycho was to be the Greenwich of the moon.

But his navigation tables were tables for the *earth.*

The problem could be solved; he knew that. By spherical trigonometry the solutions of celestial triangles on which all navigation was based could be converted to the special conditions of Luna, but it would require tedious calculation, not at all like the precalculated short cuts used by all pilots in the age of aircraft and rocket. He would have to go back to the Marc St. Hilaire method, obsolete for twenty years, after converting laboriously each piece of data from earth reference terms to moon reference terms.

Well, he could do it later, he decided, and get Cargraves to check him. The face of the moon called him.

He joined the little group huddled around the port. In front of them stretched a dun and lifeless floor, breaking into jagged hills a few miles beyond them. It was hot, glaring hot, under the oblique rays of the sun, and utterly still. The earth was not in sight; they had dropped over the rim into the unknown side in the last minutes of the impromptu landing.

Instead of the brassy sky one might expect over such a scene of blistering desert desolation, a black dome of night, studded brilliantly with stars, hung over it. At least, thought Morrie, his mind returning to his problem in navigation, it would be hard to get lost here. A man could set a course by the stars with no trouble.

"When are we going out?" demanded Art.

"Keep your shirt on," Ross told him and turned to Cargraves. "Say, Doc, that was sure a slick landing. Tell me—was that first approach just a look around on manual, or did you feed that into the automatic pilot, too?"

"Neither one, exactly." He hesitated. It had been evident from their first remarks that neither Ross nor Art had been aware of the danger, nor of his own agonizing indecision. Was it necessary to worry them with it now? He was aware that, if he did not speak, Morrie would never mention it.

That decided him. The man—*man* was the word, he now knew, not "boy"—was entitled to public credit. "Morrie made that landing," he informed them. "We had to cut out the robot and Morrie put her down."

Ross whistled.

Art said, "Huh? What did you say? Don't tell me that radar cut out—I checked it six ways."

"Your gadgets all stood up," Cargraves assured him, "but there are some things a man can do that a gadget can't. This was one of them." He elaborated what had happened.

Ross looked Morrie up and down until Morrie blushed.

"Hot Pilot I said, and Hot Pilot it is," Ross told him. "But I'm glad I didn't know." He walked aft, whistling *Danse Macabre*, off key again, and began to fiddle with his space suit.

"When do we go outside?" Art persisted.

"Practically at once, I suppose."

"Whoopee!"

"Don't get in a hurry. You might be the man with the short straw and have to stay with the ship."

"But . . . Look, Uncle, why does anybody have to stay with the ship? Nobody's going to steal it."

Cargraves hesitated. With automatic caution, he had intended always to keep at least one man in the ship, as a safety measure. On second thought there seemed no reason for it. A man inside the ship could do nothing for a man outside the ship without first donning a pressure suit and coming outside. "We'll compromise," he said. "Morrie and I —no, you and I." He realized that he could not risk both pilots at once. "You and I will go first. If it's okay, the others can follow us. All right, troops," he said, turning. "Into your space suits!"

They helped each other into them, after first applying white sunburn ointment liberally over the skin outside their goggles. It gave them an appropriate out-of-this-world appearance. Then Cargraves had them check their suits at twice normal pressure while he personally inspected their oxygen-bottle back packs.

All the while they were checking their walky-talkies; ordinary conversation could be heard, but only faintly, through the helmets as long as they were in the air of the ship; the radios were louder.

"Okay, sports," he said at last. "Art and I will go into the lock together, then proceed around to the front, where you can see us. When I give you the high sign, come on out. One last word: stay together. Don't get more than ten yards or so away from me. And remember this. When you get out there, every last one of you is going to want to see how high you can jump; I've heard you talking about it. Well, you can probably jump twenty-five or thirty feet high if you try. But don't do it!"

"Why not?" Ross's voice was strange, through the radio.

"Because if you land on your head and crack your helmet open, we'll bury you right where you fall! Come on, Morrie. No, sorry—I mean 'Art.' "

They crowded into the tiny lock, almost filling it. The motor which drove the impeller to scavenge the air from the lock whirred briefly, so little was the space left unoccupied by their bodies, then sighed and stopped. The scavenger valve clicked into place and Cargraves unclamped the outer door.

He found that he floated, rather than jumped, to the ground. Art came after him, landing on his hands and knees and springing lightly up.

"Okay, kid?"

"Swell!"

They moved around to the front, boots scuffing silently in the loose soil. He looked at it and picked up a handful to see if it looked like stuff that had been hit by radioactive blast. He was thinking of Morrie's theory. They were on the floor of a crater; that was evident, for the wall of hills extended all around them. Was it an atomic bomb crater?

He could not tell. The moon soil did have the boiled and bubbly look of atom-scorched earth, but that might have been volcanic action, or, even, the tremendous heat of the impact of a giant meteor. Well, the problem could wait.

Art stopped suddenly. "Say! Uncle, I've got to go back."

"What's the matter?"

"I forgot my camera!"

Cargraves chuckled. "Make it next time. Your subjects won't move." Art's excitement had set a new high, he decided; there was a small school of thought which believed he bathed with his camera.

Speaking of baths, Cargraves mused, I could stand one. Space travel had its drawbacks. He was beginning to dislike his own smell, particularly when it was confined in a space suit!

Ross and Morrie were waiting for them, not patiently, at the port. Their radio voices, blanked until now by the ship's sides, came clearly through the quartz. "How about it, Doc?" Ross sang out, pressing his nose to the port.

"Seems all right," they heard him say.

"Then here we come!"

"Wait a few minutes yet. I want to be sure."

"Well—okay." Ross showed his impatience, but discipline was no longer a problem. Art made faces at them, then essayed a little dance, staying close to the ground but letting each step carry him a few feet into the air—or, rather, vacuum. He floated slowly and with some grace. It was like a dance in slow motion, or a ballet under water.

When he started rising a little higher and clicking his boot heels together as he sailed, Cargraves motioned for him to stop. "Put down your flaps, chum," he cautioned, "and land. You aren't Nijinsky."

"Who's Nijinsky?"

"Never mind. Just stay planted. Keep at least one foot on the ground. Okay, Morrie," he called out, "come on out. You and Ross."

The port was suddenly deserted.

When Morrie set foot on the moon and looked around him at the flat and unchanging plain and at the broken crags beyond he felt a sudden overwhelming emotion of tragedy and of foreboding welling up inside him. "It's the bare bones," he muttered, half to himself, "the bare bones of a dead world."

"Huh?" said Ross. "Are you coming, Morrie?"

"Right behind you."

Cargraves and Art had joined them. "Where to?" asked Ross, as the captain came up.

"Well, I don't want to get too far from the ship this first time," Cargraves declared. "This place might have some dirty tricks up its sleeve that we hadn't figured on. How much pressure you guys carrying?"

"Ship pressure."

"You can cut it down to about half that without the lower pressure bothering you. It's oxygen, you know."

"Let's walk over to those hills," Morrie suggested. He pointed astern where the rim of the crater was less than half a mile from the ship. It was the sunward side and the shadows stretched from the rim to within a hundred yards or so of the ship.

"Well, part way, anyhow. That shade might feel good. I'm beginning to sweat."

"I think," said Morrie, "if I remember correctly, we ought to be able to see earth from the top of the rim. I caught a flash of it, just as we inverted. We aren't very far over on the back side."

"Just where are we?"

"I'll have to take some sights before I can report," Morrie admitted. "Some place west of *Oceanus Procellarum* and near the equator."

"I know that."

"Well, if you're in a hurry, Skipper, you had better call up the Automobile Club."

"I'm in no hurry. Injun not lost—wigwam lost. But I hope the earth is visible from there. It would be a good spot, in that case, to set up Art's antenna, not too far from the ship. Frankly, I'm opposed to moving the ship until we head back, even if we miss a chance to try to contact earth."

They were in the shadows now, to Cargraves' relief. Contrary to popular fancy, the shadows were not black, despite the lack of air-dispersed sunlight. The dazzle of the floor behind them and the glare of the hills beyond all contrived to throw quite a lot of reflected light into the shadows.

When they had proceeded some distance farther toward the hills, Cargraves realized that he was not keeping his party together too well. He had paused to examine a place, discovered by Ross, where the base rock pushed up through the waste of the desert floor, and was trying in the dim light to make out its nature, when he noticed that Morrie was not with them.

He restrained his vexation; it was entirely possible that

Morrie, who was in the lead, had not seen them stop. But he looked around anxiously.

Morrie was about a hundred yards ahead, where the first folds of the hills broke through. "Morrie!"

The figure stood up, but no answer came over the radio. He noticed then that Morrie was veering, weaving around. "Morrie! Come back here! Are you all right?"

"All right? Sure, I'm all right." He giggled.

"Well, come back here."

"Can't come back. 'M busy—I've found it!" Morrie took a careless step, bounded high in the air, came down, and staggered.

"Morrie! Stand still." Cargraves was hurrying toward him.

But he did not stand still. He began bounding around, leaping higher and higher. "I've found it!" he shrieked. "I've found it!" He gave one last bound and while he floated lazily down, he shouted, "I've found . . . the bare bones—" His voice trailed off. He lit feet first, bounced through a complete forward flip and collapsed.

Cargraves was beside him almost as he fell, having himself approached in great flying leaps.

First the helmet—no, it was not cracked. But the boy's eyes stared out sightlessly. His head lolled, his face was gray.

Cargraves gathered him up in his arms and began to run toward the *Galileo*. He knew the signs though he had seen it only in the low-pressure chamber used for pilot training—anoxia! Something had gone wrong; Morrie was starved for oxygen. He might die before he could be helped, or, still worse, he might live with his brain permanently damaged, his fine clear intellect gone.

It had happened before that way, more than once during the brave and dangerous days when man was conquering high-altitude flying.

The double burden did not slow him down. The two together, with their space suits, weighed less than seventy pounds. It was just enough to give him stability.

He squeezed them into the lock, holding Morrie close to

his chest and waited in agonizing impatience as the air hissed through the valve. All his strength would not suffice to force that door open until the pressure equalized.

Then he was in and had laid him on the deck. Morrie was still out. He tried to remove the suit with trembling, glove-hampered fingers, then hastily got out of his own suit and unclamped Morrie's helmet. No sign of life showed as the fresh air hit the patient.

Cursing bitterly he tried to give the boy oxygen directly from his suit but found that the valve on Morrie's suit, for some reason, refused to respond. He turned then to his own suit, disconnected the oxygen line and fed the raw oxygen directly to the boy's face while pushing rhythmically on his chest.

Morrie's eyes flickered and he gasped.

"What happened? Is he all right?" The other two had come through the lock while he worked.

"Maybe he is going to be all right. I don't know."

In fact he came around quickly, sat up and blinked his eyes. "Whassa matter?" he wanted to know.

"Lie down," Cargraves urged and put a hand on his shoulder.

"All right . . . hey! I'm inside."

Cargraves explained to him what had happened. Morrie blinked. "Now that's funny. I was all right, except that I was feeling exceptionally fine——"

"That's a symptom."

"Yes, I remember. But it didn't occur to me then. I had just picked up a piece of metal with a hole in it, when——"

"A *what*? You mean worked metal? Metal that some one had——"

"Yes, that's why I was so ex—" He stopped and looked puzzled. "But it couldn't have been."

"Possible. This planet might have been inhabited . . . or visited."

"Oh, I don't mean that." Morrie shrugged it off, as if it were of no importance. "I was looking at it, realizing what

133

it meant, when a little bald-headed short guy came up and
. . . but it couldn't have been."

"No," agreed Cargraves, after a short pause, "it couldn't
have been. I am afraid you were beginning to have anoxia
dreams by then. But how about this piece of metal?"

Morrie shook his head. "I don't know," he admitted. "I
remember holding it and looking at it, just as clearly as I
remember anything, ever. But I remember the little guy just
as well. He was standing there and there were others behind
him and I knew that they were the moon people. There were
buildings and trees." He stopped. "I guess that settles it."

Cargraves nodded, and turned his attention to Morrie's
oxygen pack. The valve worked properly now. There was
no way to tell what had been wrong, whether it had frosted
inside when Morrie walked on into the deeper shadows,
whether a bit of elusive dirt had clogged it, or whether
Morrie himself had shut it down too far when he had reduced pressure at Cargraves' suggestion and thereby slowly suffocated himself. But it must not happen again. He
turned to Art.

"See here, Art. I want to rig these gimmicks so that you
can't shut them off below a certain limit. Mmmm . . . no,
that isn't enough. We need a warning signal too—something
to warn the wearer if his supply stops. See what you can
dream up."

Art got the troubled look on his face that was habitual
with him whenever his gadget-conscious mind was working
at his top capacity. "I've got some peanut bulbs among
the instrument spares," he mused. "Maybe I could mount
one on the neck ring and jimmy it up so that when the flow
stopped it would—" Cargraves stopped listening; he knew
that it was only a matter of time until some unlikely but
perfectly practical new circuit would be born.

XIII "SOMEBODY IS NUTS!"

THE TOP OF THE RING OF HILLS showed them the earth, as Morrie had thought. Cargraves, Art, and Ross did the exploring, leaving Morrie back to recuperate and to work on his celestial navigation problem. Cargraves made a point of going along because he did not want the two passengers to play mountain goat on the steep crags—a great temptation under the low gravity conditions.

Also, he wanted to search over the spot where Morrie had had his mishap. Little bald men, no; a piece of metal with a hole in it—possible. If it existed it might be the first clue to the greatest discovery since man crawled up out of the darkness and became aware of himself.

But no luck—the spot was easy to find; footprints were new to this loose soil! But search as they might, they found nothing. Their failure was not quite certain, since the gloom of the crater's rim still hung over the spot. In a few days it would be daylight here; he planned to search again.

But it seemed possible that Morrie might have flung it away in his anoxia delirium, if it ever existed. It might have carried two hundred yards before it fell, and then buried itself in the loose soil.

The hill top was more rewarding. Cargraves told Art that they would go ahead with the attempt to try to beam a message back to earth . . . and then had to restrain him from running back to the ship to get started. Instead they searched for a place to install the "Dog House."

The Dog House was a small pre-fab building, now resting in sections fitting snugly to the curving walls of the *Galileo*. Art had worked on during the summer while Cargraves and Morrie were training. It was listed as a sheet-metal garage, with a curved roof, not unlike a Quonset hut, but it had the special virtue that each panel could be taken through the door of the *Galileo*.

It was not their notion simply to set it up on the face of the moon; such an arrangement would have been alternately too hot and then too cold. Instead it was to be the frame for a sort of tailor-made cave.

They found a place near the crest, between two pinnacles of rock with a fairly level floor between and of about the right size. The top of one of the crags was easily accessible and had a clear view of earth for line-of-sight, beamed transmission. There being no atmosphere, Art did not have to worry about horizon effects; the waves would go where he headed them. Having settled on the location, they returned for tools and supplies.

Cargraves and Ross did most of the building of the Dog House. It would not have been fair to Art to require him to help; he was already suffering agonies of indecision through a desire to spend all his time taking pictures and an equally strong desire to get his set assembled with which he hoped to raise earth. Morrie, at Cargraves' request, stayed on light duty for a few days, cooking, working on his navigation, and refraining from the strain of space-suit work.

The low gravitational pull made light work of moving the building sections, other materials, and tools to the spot. Each could carry over five hundred pounds, earth-weight, of the total each trip, except on the steeper portions of the trail where sheer bulk and clumsiness required them to split the loads.

First they shoveled the sandy soil about in the space between the two rocks until the ground was level enough to receive the metal floor, then they assembled the little building in place. The work went fast; wrenches alone were needed for this and the metal seemed light as cardboard. When that was done, they installed the "door," a steel drum, barrel-sized, with an air-tight gasketed head on each end.

Once the door was in place they proceeded to shovel many earth-tons of lunar soil down on top of the roof, until the space between the rock walls was filled, some three feet higher than the roof of the structure. When they were finished, nothing showed of the Dog House but the igloo-style door, sticking out between the rocky spires. The loose soil of Luna, itself a poor conductor of heat, and the vacuum spaces in it, would be their insulation.

But it was not yet air-tight. They installed portable, temporary lights, then dragged in sealed canisters and flat bales. From the canisters came sticky, tacky sheets of a rubbery plastic. This they hung like wallpaper, working as rapidly as possible in order to finish before the volatiles boiled out of the plastic. They covered ceiling, walls and floor, then from the bales they removed aluminum foil, shiny as mirrors, and slapped it on top of the plastic, all except the floor, which was covered with heavier duraluminum sheets.

It was ready for a pressure test. There were a few leaks to patch and they were ready to move in. The whole job had taken less than two "days."

The Dog House was to be Art's radio shack, but that was not all. It was to be also a storeroom for everything they could possibly spare from the ship, everything not necessary to the brief trip back. The cargo space would then be made available for specimens to take back to earth, even if the specimens were no more than country rock, lunar style.

But to Cargraves and to the three it was more than a storeroom, more than a radio shack. They were moving their personal gear into it, installing the hydroponic tank for the rhubarb plants to make the atmosphere self-refreshing, fitting it out as completely as possible for permanent residence.

To them it was a symbol of man's colonization of this planet, his intention to remain permanently, to fit it to his needs, and wrest a living from it.

Even though circumstances required them to leave it behind them in a few days, they were declaring it to be their new home, they were hanging up their hats.

They celebrated the completion of it with a ceremony which Cargraves had deliberately delayed until the Dog

House was complete. Standing in a semicircle in front of the little door, they were addressed by Cargraves:

"As commander of this expedition, duly authorized by a commission of the United Nations and proceeding in a vessel of United States registry, I take possession of this planet as a colony, on behalf of the United Nations of earth in accordance with the laws thereof and the laws of the United States. Run 'em up, Ross!"

On a short and slender staff the banner of the United Nations and the flag of the United States whipped to the top. No breeze disturbed them in that airless waste—but Ross had taken the forethought to stiffen the upper edges of each with wire; they showed their colors.

Cargraves found himself gulping as he watched the flag and banner hoisted. Privately he thought of this little hole in the ground as the first building of Luna City. He imagined that in a year or so there would be dozens of such cave dwellings, larger and better equipped, clustered around this spot. In them would live prospectors, scientists, and tough construction workers—workers who would be busy building the permanent Luna City down under the floor of the crater, while other workers installed a great rocket port up on the surface.

Nearby would be the beginning of the Cargraves Physical Laboratory, the Galileo Lunar Observatory.

He found that tears were trickling down his cheeks; he tried futilely to wipe them away—through his helmet. He caught Ross's eye and was embarrassed. "Well, sports," he said with forced heartiness, "let's get to work. Funny," he added, looking at Ross, "what effect a few little symbols can have on a man."

Ross looked from Cargraves to the bits of gay bunting. "I don't know," he said slowly. "A man isn't a collection of chemical reactions; he is a collection of ideas."

Cargraves stared. His "boys" were growing up!

"When do we start exploring?" Morrie wanted to know. "Any reason why we shouldn't get going, now that the Dog House is finished?"

"Before long, I think," Cargraves answered uncomfortably. He had been stalling Morrie's impatience for the last couple of days; Morrie was definitely disappointed that the rocket ship was not to be used, as originally planned, for point to point exploration. He felt confident that he could repeat his remarkable performance in making the first landing.

Cargraves, on the other hand, was convinced that a series of such landings would eventually result in a crash, leaving them marooned to starve or suffocate even if they were not killed in the crash. Consequently he had not budged from his decision to limit exploration to trips on foot, trips which could not be more than a few hours in duration.

"Let's see how Art is getting on," he suggested. "I don't want to leave him behind—he'll want to take pictures. On the other hand, he needs to get on with his radio work. Maybe we can rally around and furnish him with some extra hands."

"Okay." They crawled through the air lock and entered the Dog House. Art and Ross had already gone inside.

"Art," Cargraves inquired when he had taken off his clumsy suit, "how long will it be until you are ready to try out your earth sender?"

"Well, I don't know, Uncle. I never did think we could get through with the equipment we've got. If we had been able to carry the stuff I wanted——"

"You mean if we had been able to afford it," put in Ross.

"Well . . . anyhow, I've got another idea. This place is an electronics man's dream—all that vacuum! I'm going to try to gimmick up some really *big* power tubes—only they won't be tubes. I can just mount the elements out in the open without having to bother with glass. It's the easiest way to do experimental tube design anybody ever heard of."

"But even so," Morrie pointed out, "that could go on indefinitely. Doc, you've got us scheduled to leave in less than ten earth-days. Feel like stretching the stay?" he added hopefully.

"No, I don't," Cargraves stated. "Hmmm . . . Art, let's skip the transmitter problem for a moment. After all, there isn't any law that says we've got to establish radio contact with the earth. But how long would it take to get ready to receive from the earth?"

"Oh, that!" said Art. "*They* have to do all the hard work for that. Now that I've got everything up here I can finish that hook-up in a couple of hours."

"Fine! We'll whip up some lunch."

It was nearer three hours when Art announced he was ready to try. "Here goes," he said. "Stand by."

They crowded around. "What do you expect to get?" Ross asked eagerly.

Art shrugged. "Maybe nothing. NAA, or Berlin Sender, if they are beamed on us. I guess Radio Paris is the best bet, if they are still trying for us." He adjusted his controls with the vacant stare that always came over him.

They all kept very quiet. If it worked, it would be a big moment in history, and they all knew it.

He looked suddenly startled.

"Got something?"

He did not answer for a moment. Then he pushed a phone off one ear and said bitterly, "One of you guys left the power on your walky-talky."

Cargraves checked the suits himself. "No, Art, they are all dead."

Art looked around the little room. "But . . . but . . . there's nothing else it could be. Somebody is nuts!"

"What's the matter?"

" 'What's the matter?' I'm getting a power hum from somewhere and it's from somewhere around here . . . *close!*"

XIV "NO CHANCE AT ALL!"

"ARE YOU SURE?" CARGRAVES demanded.

"Of course I'm sure!"

"It's probably Radio Paris," Ross suggested. "You don't know how far away it is."

Art looked indignant. "Suppose you sit down here and try your luck, Mr. de Forrest. It was *close.* It couldn't have been an earth station."

"Feed back?"

"Don't be silly!" He tried fiddling with his dials a bit more. "It's gone now."

"Just a minute," said Cargraves. "We've got to be sure about this. Art, can you get any sort of a transmitter rigged?"

"Not very eas—yes, I can, too. The homing set is all set to go." The homing set was a low-power transmitter intended simply for communication between the Dog House and any member of the party outside in a suit.

"Gimme half a second to hook it up." It took more than half a second but shortly he was leaning toward the microphone, shouting, "Hello! Hello! Is there anybody there! Hello!"

"He must have been dreaming," Morrie said quietly to Cargraves. "There couldn't be anybody out there."

"Shut up," Art said over his shoulder and went back to calling, "Hello! Hello, hello."

His expression suddenly went blank, then he said sharply, "Speak English! Repeat!"

"What was it?" demanded Cargraves, Ross, and Morrie.

"Quiet . . . please!" Then, to the mike, "Yes, I hear you. Who is this? What? Say that again? . . . This is the Space Ship *Galileo*, Arthur Mueller transmitting. Hold on a minute." Art flipped a switch on the front of the panel. "Now go ahead. Repeat who you are."

A heavy, bass voice came out of the transmitter:

"This is Lunar Expedition Number One," the voice said. "Will you be pleased to wait one minute while I summon our leader?"

"Wait a minute," yelled Art. "Don't go away!" But the speaker did not answer.

Ross started whistling to himself. "Stop that whistling," Art demanded.

"Sorry," Ross paused, then added, "I suppose you know what this mean?"

"Huh? I don't know what anything means!"

"It means that we are too late for the senior prizes. Somebody has beaten us to it."

"Huh? How do you figure that?"

"Well, it's not certain, but it's likely."

"I'll bet we landed first."

"We'll see. Listen!" It was the speaker again, this time a different voice, lighter in timbre, with a trace of Oxford accent. "Are you there? This is Captain James Brown of the First Lunar Expedition. Is this the Rocket Ship *Galileo?*"

Cargraves leaned over to the mike. "Rocket Ship *Galileo*, Captain Cargraves speaking. Where are you?"

"Some distance away, old chap. But don't worry. We are locating you. Keep sending, please."

"Let us know where we are in reference to you."

"Do not worry about that. We will come to you. Just remain where you are and keep sending."

"What is your lunar latitude and longitude?"

The voice seemed to hesitate, then went on, "We have you located now. We can exchange details later. Good-by."

Thereafter Art shouted "hello" until he was hoarse, but there was no answer. "Better stay on the air, Art," Cargraves decided. "Ross and I will go back to the ship. That's what they will see. I don't know, though. They might not show up for a week." He mused. "This presents a lot of new problems."

"*Somebody* ought to go to the ship," Morrie pointed out,

"without waiting. They may be just coming in for a landing. They may show up any time.'

"I don't think it was ship transmission," said Art, then turned back to his microphone.

Nevertheless it was decided that Cargraves and Ross would go back to the ship. They donned their suits and crawled through the air lock, and had no more than started down the steep and rocky slope when Ross saw the rocket.

He did not hear it, naturally, but he had glanced back to see if Cargraves was behind him. "Look!" he called into his helmet mike, and pointed.

The ship approached them from the west, flying low and rather slowly. The pilot was riding her on her jet, for the blast shot more downward than to the stern. "We had better hurry!" Ross shouted, and went bounding ahead.

But the rocket did not come in for a landing. It nosed down, forward jets driving hard against the fall, directly toward the *Galileo*. At an altitude of not more than five hundred feet the pilot kicked her around, belly first, and drove away on his tail jet.

Where the *Galileo* lay, there was a flash, an utterly silent explosion, and a cloud of dust which cleared rapidly away in the vacuum. The sound reached them through their feet, after a long time—it seemed to them.

The *Galileo* lay on her side, a great gaping hole in her plates. The wound stretched from shattered view port to midships.

Cargraves stood perfectly still, staring at the unbelievable. Ross found his voice first. "They gave us no chance," he said, shaking both fists at the sky. "No chance at all!"

XV   WHAT POSSIBLE REASON?

HE TURNED AND STUMBLED back up the slope to where Cargraves still stood forlorn and motionless. "Did you see that, Doc?" he demanded. "Did you see that? The dirty rats bombed us—they bombed us. Why? Why, Doc? Why would they do such a thing?"

Tears were streaming down his face. Cargraves patted him clumsily. "I don't know," he said slowly. "I don't know," he repeated, still trying to readjust himself to the shock.

"Oh, I want to kill somebody!"

"So do I." Cargraves turned away suddenly. "Maybe we will. Come on—we've got to tell the others." He started up the slope.

But Art and Morrie were already crawling out of the lock when they reached it. "What happened?" Morrie demanded. "We felt a quake."

Cargraves did not answer directly. "Art, did you turn off your transmitter?"

"Yes, but what happened?"

"Don't turn it on again. It will lead them to us here." He waved a hand out at the floor of the crater. "Look!"

It took a minute or two for what they saw to sink in. Then Art turned helplessly to Cargraves. "But, Uncle," he pleaded, "what happened? Why did the ship blow up?"

"They blitzed us," Cargraves said savagely. "They bombed us out. If we had been aboard they would have killed us. That's what they meant to do."

"But why?"

"No possible reason. They didn't want us here." He refrained from saying what he felt to be true: that their unknown enemy had failed only temporarily in his intent to kill. A quick death by high explosive would probably be a blessing compared with what he felt was in store for them . . . marooned . . . on a dead and airless planet.

How long would they last? A month? Two months? Better by far if the bomb had hit them.

Morrie turned suddenly back toward the lock. "What are you doing, Morrie?"

"Going to get the guns!"

"Guns are no good to us."

But Morrie had not heard him. His antenna was already shielded by the metal drum.

Ross said, "I'm not sure that guns are no good, Doc."

"Huh? How do you figure?"

"Well, what are they going to do next? Won't they want to see what they've done? They didn't even see the bomb hit; they were jetting away."

"Yes?"

"If they land we'll hijack their ship!"

Art came up closer. "Huh? Hey, Ross, that's tellin' 'em! We'll get them! We'll show them! Murderers!" His words tumbled over one another, squeaking and squawking in their radios.

"We'll try!" Cargraves decided suddenly. "We'll try. If they land we won't go down without a fight. We can't be any worse off than we are." He was suddenly unworried; the prospect of a gun fight, something new to his experience, did not upset him further. It cheered him. "Where do you think we ought to hide, Ross? In the *Galileo?*"

"If we have— *There they come!*" The rocket had suddenly appeared over the far rim.

"Where's Morrie?"

"Here." He came up from behind them, burdened with the two rifles and the revolver. "Here, Ross, you take . . . *hey!*" He had caught sight of the strangers' rocket. "We've got to hurry," he said.

But the rocket did not land. It came down low, dipping below the level of the crater's rim, then scooted on its tail across near the wreckage of the *Galileo*, up, out, and away.

"And we didn't even get a crack at them," Morrie said bitterly.

"Not yet," Ross answered, "but I think they'll be back. This was a second bombing run, sure as anything, in case they missed the first time. They'll still come back to see what they've done. How about it, Doc?"

"I think they will," Cargraves decided. "They will want to look over our ship and to kill us off if they missed any of us. But we don't go to the *Galileo*."

"Why not?"

"We haven't time. They will probably turn as fast as they can check themselves, come back and land. We might be caught out in the open."

"That's a chance we'll have to take."

It was decided for them. The rocket appeared again from the direction it had gone. This time it was plainly a landing trajectory. "Come on!" shouted Cargraves, and went careening madly down the slope.

The rocket landed about halfway between the *Galileo* and the shadows, now close to the foot of the hills, for the sun had climbed four "days" higher in the sky. The ship was noticeably smaller than the *Galileo* even at that distance.

Cargraves did not notice such details. His immediate intent was to reach the door of the craft before it opened, to be ready to grapple with them as they came out.

But his good sense came to his aid before he was out in the sunlight. He realized he had no gun. Morrie had kept one, Ross had the other, and Art was waving the revolver around. He paused just short of the dazzling, sunlighted area. "Hold it," he ordered. "I don't think they have seen us. I don't think they will—yet."

"What are your plans?" Morrie demanded.

"Wait for them to get out, then rush the ship—after they get well away from it. Wait for my signal."

"Can't they hear us?"

"Maybe. If they are on this frequency, we're goners. Switch off your talkies, everybody." He did so himself; the sudden silence was chilling.

The rocket was almost tail towards them. He now saw three suit-clad figures pile out from a door that swung out from the side. The first looked around briefly, but he appeared not to see them. Since it was almost certain that he was wearing sun goggles, it was doubtful if he could see much inside the shadows.

He motioned to the other two and moved toward the *Galileo,* using a long, loping gallop that the *Galileo's* crew had learned was the proper way to walk on the moon. That alone was enough to tell Cargraves that these men, their enemies, were not grounding on the moon for the first time.

Cargraves let them get all the way to the *Galileo,* and, in fact, to disappear behind it, before he got up from where he had been crouching. "Come on!" he yelled into a dead microphone, and slammed ahead in great leaps that took him fifty feet at a stride.

The outer door of the lock stood open. He swarmed into it and closed it after him. It clamped by means of a wheel mounted in its center; the operation was obvious. That done he looked around. The tiny lock was dimly illuminated by a pane of glass set in the inner door. In this feeble light he looked and felt for what he needed next—the spill valve for air.

He found it and heard the air hissing into the compartment. He leaned his weight against the inner door and waited.

Suddenly it gave way; he was in the rocket and blinking his eyes.

There was a man still seated in the pilot's chair. He turned his head, and appeared to say comething. Cargraves could not hear it through his helmet and was not interested. Taking all advantage of the low gravity he dived at the man and grappled him about the head and shoulders.

The man was too surprised to put up much of a fight—not that it would have mattered; Cargraves felt ready to fight anything up to and including tigers.

He found himself banging the man's head against the soft padding of the acceleration chair. That, he realized, was no good. He drew back a gauntleted fist and buried it in the pit of the man's stomach.

The man grunted and seemed to lose interest. Cargraves threw a short jab straight to the unguarded chin. No further treatment was needed. Cargraves pushed him down to the floor, noticing without interest that the belt of his victim carried a holster with what appeared to be a heavy-caliber Mauser, and then stood on him. He looked out the conning port.

There was a figure collapsed on the ground near the broken bow of the *Galileo*, whether friend or foe it was impossible to say. But another was standing over him and concerning him there was no doubt. It was not alone the unfamiliar cut of his space suit, it was the pistol in his hand. He was firing in the direction of the rocket in which Cargraves stood.

He saw the blaze of a shot, but no answering report. Another shot followed it—and this one almost deafened him; it struck the ship containing him, making it ring like a giant bell.

He was in a dilemma. He wanted very urgently to join the fight; the weapon on the person of his disabled opponent offered a way. Yet he could not leave his prisoner inside the ship while he went out, nor did he, even in the heat of fighting, have any stomach for killing an unconscious man.

He had already decided, in the space of a breath, to slug his man heavily and get outside, when the fast drama beyond the port left him no time. The space-suited stranger at the bow of the *Galileo* was suddenly without a helmet. Around his neck was only a jagged collar.

He dropped his pistol and clutched at his face. He stood there for a moment, as if puzzled by his predicament, took two hesitant steps forward, and sank gently to the ground.

He thrashed around a bit but did not get up. He was still convulsing when a third man appeared around the end of the ship. He did not last long. He appeared confused, unable to comprehend the turn of events, which was quite likely, in view of the ghostly stillness of the gun fight. It was entirely possible that he never knew what hit him, nor why. He was still reaching for his iron when he was struck twice, first in the chest and the second shot lower down.

He bowed forward, until his helmet touched the ground, then collapsed.

Cargraves heard a noise behind him. Snatching the gun he had taken to the ready, and turning, he watched the door of the air lock open.

It was Art, wild-eyed and red. "Any more in here?" the boy called out to him, while swinging his revolver in a wide arc. His voice reached Cargraves faintly, muffled by their two helmets.

"No. Turn on your radio," he shouted back, then realized his own was still off. Switching it on, he repeated his statement.

"Mine *is* on," Art replied. "I turned it on while the lock filled. How are they doing outside?"

"All right, it looks like. Here, you guard this guy." He pointed down at his feet. "I'm going outside."

But it was unnecessary. The lock opened again and both Ross and Morrie bulged out of it. Cargraves wondered absently how the two had managed to squeeze into that coffin-like space.

"Need any help?" demanded Morrie.

"No. It doesn't look like you guys did, either."

"We ambushed 'em," Ross said jubilantly. "Hid in the shadow of the ship and picked 'em off as they showed up. All but the second one. He darn near got us before we got him. Do you know," he went on conversationally, as if he had spent a lifetime shooting it out, "it's almost impossible to sight a gun when you're wearing one of these fish bowls over your head?"

"Hmm . . . You made out all right."

"Pure luck. Morrie was shooting from the hip."

"I was not," Morrie denied. "I aimed and squeezed off every shot."

Cargraves cautioned them to keep an eye on the prisoner,

as he wanted to take a look around outside. "Why," demanded Art, "bother to guard him? Shoot him and chuck him out, I say."

"Cool down," Cargraves told him. "Shooting prisoners isn't civilized."

Art snorted. "Is *he* civilized?"

"Shut up, Art. Morrie—take charge." He shut himself in the air lock.

The examination took little time. Two of the strangers had received wounds which would have been fatal in any case, it seemed to him, but their suits were deflated in any event. The third, whose helmet had been struck, was equally beyond help. His eyes bulged sightlessly at the velvet sky. Blood from his nose still foamed. He was gone—drowned in vacuum.

He went back to the little ship, without even a glance at the dismal pile of junk that had been the sleekly beautiful *Galileo*.

Back in the ship, he threw himself in one of the acceleration chairs and sighed. "Not so bad," he said. "We've got a ship."

"That's what you think," Art said darkly. "Take a look at that instrument board."

XVI THE SECRET BEHIND THE MOON

"What!" said Cargraves and looked where he was pointing.

"This is no space ship," Art said bitterly. "This thing is a jeep. Look at that." He indicated two gauges. One was marked *SAUERSTOFF*, the other *ALKOHOL*. "Oxygen and alcohol. This thing is just a kiddy wagon."

"Maybe those are just for the maneuvering jets," Cargraves answered, not very hopefully.

"Not a chance, Doc," Ross put in. "I've already given her the once-over, with Art translating the Jerry talk for me. Besides, did you notice that this boat hasn't any wings of any sort? It's purely a station wagon for the moon. Look—we've got company."

The prisoner had opened his eyes and was trying to sit up.

Cargraves grabbed him by a shoulder, yanked him to his feet, and shoved him into the chair he had just vacated. "Now, you," he snapped. "Talk!"

The man looked dazed and did not answer. "Better try German on him, Uncle," Art suggested. "The labels are all in German."

Cargraves reached far back into his technical education and shifted painfully to German. "What is your name?"

"My name is Friedrich Lenz, sergeant-technician of the second class. To whom am I speaking?"

"Answer the questions you are asked. Why did you bomb our ship?"

"In line of duty. I was ordered."

"That is not a reason. Why did you bomb a peaceful ship?"

The man simply looked sullen. "Very well," Cargraves went on, still speaking in German. "Get the air lock open, Art. We'll throw this trash out on the face of the moon."

The self-styled sergeant-technician suddenly began talking very rapidly. Cargraves wrinkled his forehead. "Art," he said, returning to English, "you'll have to help me out. He's slinging it too fast for me."

"And translate!" protested Ross. "What does he say?"

"I'll try," Art agreed, then shifted to German. "Answer the question over again. Speak slowly."

"*Ja*—" the man agreed, addressing his words to Cargraves.

" 'Herr Kapitän!' " Art thundered at him.

" 'Ja, Herr Kapitän,' " the man complied respectfully, "I was trying to explain to you—" He went on at length.

Art translated when he paused. "He says that he is part of the crew of this rocket. He says that it was commanded by Lieutenant—I didn't catch the name; it's one of the guys we shot—and that they were ordered by their leader to seek out and bomb a ship at this location. He says that it was not a . . . uh, a *wanton* attack because it was an act of war."

"War?" demanded Ross. "What in thunder does he mean, 'war'? There's no war. It was sheer attempted murder."

Art spoke with the prisoner again.

"He says that there is a war, that there always has been a war. He says that there will always be war until the National Socialist Reich is victorious." He listened for a moment. "He says that the Reich will live a thousand years."

Morrie used some words that Cargraves had never heard him use before. "Ask him how he figures that one."

"Never mind," put in Cargraves. "I'm beginning to get the picture." He addressed the Nazi directly. "How many are there in your party, how long has it been on the moon, and where is your base?"

Presently Art said, "He claims he doesn't have to answer questions of that sort, under international law."

"Hummph! You might tell him that the laws of warfare went out when war was abolished. But never mind—tell him that, if he wants to claim prisoner-of-war privileges, we'll give him his freedom, right now!" He jerked a thumb at the air lock.

He had spoken in English, but the prisoner understood the gesture. After that he supplied details readily.

He and his comrades had been on the moon for nearly three months. They had an underground base about thirteen miles west of the crater in which the shattered *Galileo* lay. There was one rocket at the base, much larger than the *Galileo*, and it, too, was atom-powered. He regarded himself as a member of the army of the Nazi Reich. He did not know why the order had been given to blast the *Galileo,* but he supposed that it was an act of military security to protect their plans.

"What plans?"

He became stubborn again. Cargraves actually opened the inner door of the lock, not knowing himself how far he was prepared to go to force information out of the man, when the Nazi cracked.

The plans were simple—the conquest of the entire earth. The Nazis were few in number, but they represented some of the top military, scientific, and technical brains from Hitler's crumbled empire. They had escaped from Germany, established a remote mountain base, and there had been working ever since for the redemption of the Reich. The sergeant appeared not to know where the base was; Cargraves questioned him closely. Africa? South America? An island? But all that he could get out of him was that it was a long submarine trip from Germany.

But it was the objective, *der Tag,* which left them too stunned to worry about their own danger. The Nazis had atom bombs, but, as long as they were still holed up in their secret base on earth, they dared not act, for the UN had them, too, and in much greater quantity.

But when they achieved space flight, they had an answer. They would sit safely out of reach on the moon and destroy the cities of earth one after another by guided missiles launched from the moon, until the completely helpless nations of earth surrendered and pleaded for mercy.

The announcement of the final plan brought another flash of arrogance back into their prisoner. "And you cannot stop it," he concluded. "You may kill me, but you cannot stop it! *Heil dem Führer!*"

"Mind if I spit in his eye, Doc?" Morrie said conversationally.

"Don't waste it," Cargraves counseled. "Let's see if we can think ourselves out of this mess. Any suggestions?" He hauled the prisoner out of the chair and made him lie face down on the deck. Then he sat down on him. "Go right ahead," he urged. "I don't think he understand two words of English. How about it, Ross?"

"Well," Ross answered, "it's more than just saving our necks now. We've *got* to stop them. But the notion of tackling fifty men with two rifles and two pistols sounds like a job for Tarzan or Superman. Frankly, I don't know how to start."

"Maybe we can start by scouting them out. Thirteen miles isn't much. Not on the moon."

"Look," said Art, "in a day or two I might have a transmitter rigged that would raise earth. What we need is reinforcements."

"How are they going to get here?" Ross wanted to know. "We had the only space ship—except for the Nazis."

"Yes, but listen—Doc's plans are still available. You left full notes with Ross's father—didn't you, Doc? They can get busy and rebuild some more and come up here and blast those skunks out."

"That might be best," Cargraves answered. "We can't afford to miss, that's sure. They could raid the earth base of the Nazis first thing and then probably bust this up in a few weeks, knowing that our ship did work and having our plans."

Morrie shook his head. "It's all wrong. We've got to get at them *right now*. No delay at all, just the way they smashed us. Suppose it takes the UN six weeks to get there. Six weeks might be too long. Three weeks might be too long. A week might be too long. An atom war could be all over in a day."

"Well, let's ask our pal if he knows when they expect to strike, then," Ross offered.

Morrie shook his head and stopped Art from doing so. "Useless. We'll never get a chance to build a transmitter. They'll be swarming over this crater like reporters around a murder trial. Look—they'll be here any minute. *Don't you think they'll miss this rocket?*"

"Oh, my gosh!" It was Art. Ross added, "What time is it, Doc?"

To their complete amazement it was only forty minutes

from the time the *Galileo* had been bombed. It had seemed like a full day.

It cheered them up a little but not much. The prisoner had admitted that the rocket they were in was the only utility, short-jump job. And the Nazi space ship—the *Wotan*, he termed it—would hardly be used for search. Perhaps they had a few relatively free hours.

"But I still don't see it," Cargraves admitted. "Two guns and two pistols—four of us. The odds are too long—and we can't afford to lose. I know you sports aren't afraid to die, but we've got to *win*."

"Why," inquired Ross, "does it have to be rifles?"

"What else?"

"This crate bombed us. I'll bet it carries more than one bomb."

Cargraves looked startled, then turning to the prisoner, spoke rapidly in German. The prisoner gave a short reply. Cargraves nodded and said, "Morrie, do you think you could fly this clunker?"

"I could sure make a stab at it."

"Okay. You are it. We'll make Joe Masterrace here take it off, with a gun in his ribs, and you'll have to feel her out. You won't get but one chance and no practice. Now let's take a look at the bomb controls."

The bomb controls were simple. There was no bombsight, as such. The pilot drove the ship on a straight diving course and kicked it out just before his blast upwards. There was a gadget to expel the bomb free of the ship; it continued on the ship's previous trajectory. Having doped it out, they checked with the Nazi pilot who gave them the same answers they had read in the mechanism.

There were two pilot seats and two passenger seats, directly behind the pilot seats. Morrie took one pilot seat; the Nazi the other. Ross sat behind Morrie, while Cargraves sat with Art in his lap, one belt around both. This squeezed Art up close to the back of the Nazi's chair, which was good, for Art reached around and held a gun in the Nazi's side.

"All set, Morrie?"

"All set. I make one pass to get my bearings and locate the mouth of their hideaway. Then I come back and give 'em the works."

"Right. Try not to hit their rocket ship, if you can. It would be nice to go home. Blast off! *Achtung! Aufstieg!*"

The avengers raised ground.

"How is it going?" Cargraves shouted a few moments later.

"Okay!" Morrie answered, raising his voice to cut through the roar. "I could fly her down a chimney. There's the hill ahead, I think—there!"

The silvery shape of the *Wotan* near the hill they were shooting towards put a stop to any doubts. It appeared to be a natural upthrust of rock, quite different from the craters, and lay by itself a few miles out in one of the "seas."

They were past it and Morrie was turning, blasting heavily to kill his momentum, and pressing them hard into their seats. Art fought to steady the revolver without firing it.

Morrie was headed back on his bombing run, coming in high for his dive. Cargraves wondered if Morrie had actually seen the air lock of the underground base; he himself had had no glimpse of it.

There was no time left to wonder. Morrie was diving; they were crushed against the pads as he fought a moment later to recover from the dive, kicking her up and blasting. They hung for a second and Cargraves thought that Morrie had played it too fine in his anxiety to get in a perfect shot; he braced himself for the crash.

Then they were up. When he had altitude, Morrie kicked her over again, letting his jet die. They dropped, view port down, with the ground staring at them.

They could see the splash of dust and sand still rising. Suddenly there was a *whoosh* from the middle of it, a mighty blast of air, bits of debris, and more sand. It cleared at once in the vacuum of that plain, and they saw the open wound, a black hole leading downward.

He had blown out the air lock with a bull's-eye.

Morrie put her down to Cargraves' plan, behind the *Wotan* and well away from the hole. "Okay, Doc!"

"Good. Now let's run over the plan—I don't want any slip-up. Ross comes with me. You and Art stay with the jeep. We will look over the *Wotan* first, then scout out the base. If we are gone longer than thirty minutes, you must assume that we are dead or captured. No matter what happens, under no circumstances whatever are you to leave this rocket. If any one comes toward you, blast off. Don't even let us come near you unless we are by ourselves. Blast off. You've got one more bomb—you know what to do with it."

Morrie nodded. "Bomb the *Wotan*. I hate to do that." He stared wistfully at the big ship, their one chain to the earth.

"But you've got to. You and Art have got to run for it, then, and get back to the Dog House and hole up. It'll be your business, Art, to manage somehow or other to throw together a set that can get a message back to earth. That's your only business, both of you. Under no circumstances are you to come back here looking for Ross and me. If you stay holed up, they may not find you for weeks—and that will give you your chance, the *earth's* chance. Agreed?"

Morrie hesitated. "Suppose we get a message through to earth. How about it then?"

Cargraves thought for a moment, then replied, "We can't stand here jawing—there's work to be done. If you get a message through with a reply that makes quite clear that they believe you and are getting busy, then you are on your own. But I advise you not to take any long chances. If we aren't back here in thirty minutes, you probably can't help us." He paused for a moment and decided to add one more thing—the boy's personal loyalty had made him doubtful about one point. "You know, don't you, that when it comes to dropping that bomb, if you do, you must drop it where it has to go, even if Ross and I are standing on your target?"

"I suppose so."

"Those are orders, Morrie."

"I understand them."

"Morrie!"

"Aye aye, Captain!"

"Very well, sir—that's better. Art, Morrie is in charge Come on, Ross."

Nothing moved on the rocket field. The dust of the bomb ing, with no air to hold it up, had dissipated completely The broken air lock showed dark and still across the field near them the sleek and mighty *Wotan* crouched silent and untended.

Cargraves made a circuit of the craft, pistol ready in his gloved fist, while Ross tailed him, armed with one of the Garands. Ross kept well back, according to plan.

Like the *Galileo*, the *Wotan* had but one door, on the port side just abaft the conning compartment. He motioned Ross to stay back, then climbed a little metal ladder or staircase and tried the latch. To his surprise the ship was not locked—then he wondered why he was surprised. Locks were for cities.

While the pressure in the air chamber equalized, he un-snapped from his belt a flashlight he had confiscated from the Nazi jeep rocket and prepared to face whatever lay be-yond the door. When the door sighed open, he dropped low and to one side, then shot his light around the compart-ment. Nothing . . . nobody.

The ship was empty of men from stem to stern. It was almost too much luck. Even if it had been a rest period, or even if there had been no work to do in the ship, he had expected at least a guard on watch.

However a guard on watch would mean one less pair of hands for work . . . and this was the moon, where every pair of hands counted for a hundred or a thousand on earth. Men were at a premium here; it was more likely, he con-cluded, that their watch was a radar, automatic and un-sleeping. Probably with a broad-band radio alarm as well, he thought, remembering how promptly their own call had been answered the very first time they had ever sent any-thing over the rim of their crater.

He went through a passenger compartment equipped with

dozens of acceleration bunks, through a hold, and farther aft. He was looking for the power plant.

He did not find it. Instead he found a welded steel bulkhead with no door of any sort. Puzzled, he went back to the control station. What he found there puzzled him still more. The acceleration chairs were conventional enough; some of the navigational instruments were common types and all of them not too difficult to figure out; but the controls simply did not make sense.

Although this bewildered him, one point was very clear. The Nazis had not performed the nearly impossible task of building a giant space ship in a secret hide-out, any more than he and the boys had built the *Galileo* singlehanded. In each case it had been a job of conversion plus the installation of minor equipment.

For the *Wotan* was one of the finest, newest, biggest ships ever to come out of Detroit!

The time was getting away from him. He had used up seven minutes in his prowl through the ship. He hurried out and rejoined Ross. "Empty," he reported, saving the details for later; "let's try their rat hole." He started loping across the plain.

They had to pick their way carefully through the rubble at the mouth of the hole. Since the bomb had not been an atom bomb but simply ordinary high explosive, they were in no danger of contamination, but they were in danger of slipping, sliding, falling, into the darkness.

Presently the rubble gave way to an excellent flight of stairs leading deep into the moon. Ross flashed his torch around. The walls, steps, and ceiling were covered with some tough lacquer, sprayed on to seal the place. The material was transparent, or nearly so, and they could see that it covered carefully fitted stonework.

"Went to a lot of trouble, didn't they?" Ross remarked.

"Keep quiet!" answered Cargraves.

More than two hundred feet down the steep passageway ended, and they came to another door, not an air lock, but intended apparently as an air-tight safety door. It had not kept the owners safe; the blast followed by a sudden letting up of normal pressure had been too much for it. It was jammed in place but so bulged and distorted that there was room for them to squeeze through.

There was some light in the room beyond. The blast had broken most of the old-fashioned bulbs the Nazis had used, but here and there a light shone out, letting them see that they were in a large hall. Cargraves went cautiously ahead.

A room lay to the right from the hall, through an ordinary non-air-tight door, now hanging by one hinge. In it they found the reason why the field had been deserted when they had attacked.

The room was a barrack room; the Nazis had died in their bunks. "Night" and "day" were arbitrary terms on the moon, in so far as the working times and eating times and sleeping times of men are concerned. The Nazis were on another schedule; they had had the bad luck to be sleeping when Morrie's bomb had robbed them of their air.

Cargraves stayed just long enough in the room to assure himself that all were dead. He did not let Ross come in at all. There was some blood, but not much, being mostly bleeding from mouths and bulging eyes. It was not this that caused his squeamish consideration; it was the expressions which were frozen on their dead faces.

He got out before he got sick.

Ross had found something. "Look here!" he demanded.

Cargraves looked. A portion of the wall had torn away under the sudden drop in pressure and had leaned crazily into the room. It was a metal panel, instead of the rock masonry which made up the rest of the walls. Ross had pulled and pried at it to see what lay behind, and was now playing his light into the darkness behind it.

It was another corridor, lined with carefully dressed and fitted stones. But here the stone had not been covered with the sealing lacquer.

"I wonder why they sealed it off after they built it?" Ross wanted to know. "Do you suppose they have stuff stored down there? Their A-bombs maybe?"

Cargraves studied the patiently fitted stones stretching away into the unfathomed darkness. After a long time he answered softly, "Ross, you haven't discovered a Nazi storeroom. You have discovered the homes of the people of the moon."

XVII   "—UNTIL WE ROT—"

FOR ONCE ROSS WAS ALMOST as speech-bound as Art. When he was able to make his words behave he demanded, "Are you sure? Are you sure, Doc?"

Cargraves nodded. "As sure as I can be at this time. I wondered why the Nazis had built such a deep and extensive a base and why they had chosen to use fitted stone masonry. It would be hard to do, working in a space suit. But I assigned it to their reputation for doing things the hard way, what they call 'efficiency.' I should have known better." He peered down the mysterious, gloomy corridor. "Certainly this was not built in the last few months."

"How long ago, do you think?"

"How long? How long is a million years? How long is ten million years? I don't know—I have trouble imagining a thousand years. Maybe we'll never know."

Ross wanted to explore. Cargraves shook his head. "We can't go chasing rabbits. This is wonderful, the biggest thing in ages. But it will wait. Right now," he said, glancing at his watch, "we've got eleven minutes to finish the job and get back up to the surface—or things will start happening up there!"

He covered the rest of the layout at a fast trot, with Ross guarding his rear from the central hall. He found the radio "shack," with a man dead in his phones, and noted that the equipment did not appear to have suffered much damage when the whirlwind of escaping air had slammed out of the place. Farther on, an arsenal contained bombs for the jeep, and rifles, but no men.

He found the storeroom for the guided missiles, more than two hundred of them, although the cradles were only half used up. The sight of them should have inspired terror, knowing as he did that each represented a potentially dead and blasted city, but he had no time for it. He rushed on.

There was a smaller room, well furnished, which seemed to be sort of a wardroom and common room for the officers. It was there that he found a Nazi who was not as the others.

He was sprawled face down and dressed in a space suit. Although he did not move Cargraves approached him very cautiously.

The man was either dead or unconscious. However, he did not have the grimace of death on his face and his suit was still under pressure. Wondering what to do, Cargraves knelt over him. There was a pistol in his belt; Cargraves took it and stuck it in his own.

He could feel no heart-beat through the heavy suit and his own gauntlet, nor could he listen for it, while wearing a helmet himself.

His watched showed five minutes of the agreed time left; whatever he did must be done fast. He grappled the limp form by the belt and dragged it along.

"What have you got there?" Ross demanded.

"Souvenir. Let's get going. No time." He saved his breath for the climb. The sixty-pound weight that he and his burden made, taken together, flew up the stairs six at a time. At the top his watch still showed two minutes to go. "Leg it out to the jeep," he commanded Ross. "I can't take this item there, or Morrie may decide it's a trap. Meet me in the *Wotan*. Get going!" Heaving his light burden over one shoulder, he set out for the big ship at a gallop.

Once inside he put his load down and took the man out

of his space suit. The body was warm but seemed dead. However, he found he could detect a faint heart-beat. He was starting an artificial respiration when the boys piled out of the lock.

"Hi," he said, "who wants to relieve me here? I don't know much about it."

"Why bother?" asked Morrie.

Cargraves paused momentarily and looked at him quizzically. "Well, aside from the customary reasons you have been brought up to believe in, he might be more use to us alive than dead."

Morrie shrugged. "Okay, I'll take over." He dropped to his knees, took Cargraves' place, and started working.

"Did you bring them up to date?" Cargraves asked Ross.

"I gave them a quick sketch. Told them the place seemed to be ours and I told them what we found—the ruins."

"Not very ruined," Cargraves remarked.

"Look, Uncle," demanded Art. "Can I go down there? I've got to get some pictures."

"Pictures can wait," Cargraves pointed out. "Right now we've got to find out how this ship works. As soon as we get the hang of it, we head back. That comes first."

"Well, sure," Art conceded, "but . . . after all—I mean. No pictures at all?"

"Well . . . Let's put it this way. It may take Ross and Morrie and me, not to mention yourself, quite some time to figure out how they handle this craft. There might be twenty minutes when we could spare you. In the meantime, table the motion. Come on, Ross. By the way, what did you do with the prisoner?"

"Oh, him," Morrie answered, "we tied him up and left him."

"Huh? Suppose he gets loose? He might steal the rocket."

"He won't get loose. I tied him myself and I took a personal interest in it. Anyhow he won't try to get away—no space suit, no food. That baby knows his chance of living to a ripe old age depends on us and he doesn't want to spoil ."

"That's right, Uncle," Art agreed. "You should have heard what he promised me."

"Good enough, I guess," Cargraves conceded. "Come on, Ross." Morrie went on with his job, with Art to spell him.

Cargraves returned, with Ross, to the central compartment a few minutes later. "Isn't that pile of meat showing signs of life yet?" he asked.

"No. Shall I stop?"

"I'll relieve you. Sometimes they come to after an hour or more. Two of you go over to the jeep with an additional space suit and bring back Sergeant What's-his-name. Ross and I are as much in the dark as ever," he explained. "The sergeant bloke is a pilot. We'll sweat it out of him."

He had no more than gotten firmly to work when the man under him groaned. Morrie turned back at the lock. "Go ahead," Cargraves confirmed. "Ross and I can handle this guy."

The Nazi stirred and moaned. Cargraves turned him over. The man's eyelids flickered, showing bright blue eyes. He stared up at Cargraves. "How do you do?" he said in a voice like a stage Englishman. "May I get up from here?"

Cargraves backed away and let him up. He did not help him.

The man looked around. Ross stood silently, covering him with a Garand. "That isn't necessary, really," the Nazi protested. Ross glanced at Cargraves but continued to cover the prisoner. The man turned to Cargraves. "Whom have I the honor of addressing?" he asked. "Is it Captain Cargraves of the *Galileo*?"

"That's right. Who are you?"

"I am Helmut von Hartwick, Lieutenant Colonel, Elite Guard." He pronounced lieutenant "leftenant."

"Okay, Helmut, suppose you start explaining yourself. Just what is the big idea?"

The self-styled colonel laughed. "Really, old man, there isn't much to explain, is there? You seem to have eluded us somehow and placed me at a disadvantage. I can see that."

"You had better see that, but that is not what I mean.

and that is not enough." Cargraves hesitated. The Nazi had him somewhat baffled; he did not act at all like a man who has just come out of a daze. Perhaps he had been playing 'possum—if so, for how long?

Well, it did not matter, he decided. The Nazi was still his prisoner. "Why did you order my ship bombed?"

"Me? My dear chap, why do you think *I* ordered it?"

"Because you sound just like the phony English accent we heard over our radio. You called yourself 'Captain James Brown.' I don't suppose there is more than one fake Englishman in this crowd of gangsters."

Von Hartwick raised his eyebrows. " 'Gangsters' is a harsh term, old boy. Hardly good manners. But you are correct on one point; I was the only one of my colleagues who had enjoyed the questionable advantage of attending a good English school. I'll ask you not to call my accent 'phony.' But, even if I did borrow the name 'Captain James Brown,' that does not prove that I ordered your ship bombed. That was done under the standing orders of our Leader—a necessary exigency of war. I was not personally responsible."

"I think you are a liar on both counts. I don't think you ever attended an English school; you probably picked up that fake accent from Lord Haw-Haw, or from listening to the talkies. And your Leader did not order us bombed, because he did not know we were there. You ordered it, just as soon as you could take a bearing on us, as soon as you found out we were here."

The Nazi spread his hands, palms down, and looked pained. "Really, you Americans are so ready to jump to conclusions. Do you truly think that I could fuel a rocket, call its crew, and equip it for bombing, all in ten minutes? My only function was to report your location."

"You expected us, then?"

"Naturally. If a stupid radarman had not lost you when you swung into your landing orbit, we would have greeted you much sooner. Surely you don't think that we would have established a military base without preparing to defend it? We plan, we plan for everything. That is why we will win."

Cargraves permitted himself a thin smile. "You don't seem to have planned this."

The Nazi tossed it off. "In war there are setbacks. One expects them."

"Do you call it 'war' to bomb an unarmed, civilian craft without even a warning?"

Hartwick looked pained. "Please, my dear fellow! It ill befits you to split hairs. You seemed to have bombed *us* without warning. I myself would not be alive this minute had I not had the good fortune to be just removing my suit when you struck. I assure you *I* had no warning. As for your claim to being a civilian, unarmed craft, I think it very strange that the *Galileo* was able to blast our base if you carried nothing more deadly than a fly swatter. You Americans amaze me. You are always so ready to condemn others for the very things you do yourselves."

Cargraves was at a loss for words at the blind illogic of the speech. Ross looked disgusted; he seemed about to say something. Cargraves shook his head at him.

"That speech," he announced, "had more lies, half-truths, and twisted statements per square inch than anything you've said yet. But I'll put you straight on one point: the *Galileo* didn't bomb your base; she's wrecked. But your men were careless. We seized your rocket and turned your own bombs on you——"

"*Idioten!*"

"They *were* stupid, weren't they? The Master Race usually is stupid when it comes to a showdown. But you claimed we bombed you without warning. That is not true; you had all the warning you were entitled to and more. You struck the first blow. It's merely your own cocksureness that led you to think we couldn't, or wouldn't strike back."

Von Hartwick started to speak. "Shut up!" Cargraves said sharply. "I'm tired of your nonsense. Tell me how you happen to have this American ship. Make it good."

"Oh, that! We bought it."

"Don't be silly."

"I am not being silly. Naturally we did not walk in and place an order for one military space ship, wrapped and delivered. The transaction passed through several hands and eventually our friends delivered to us what we needed."

Cargraves thought rapidly. It was possible; something of the sort had to be true. He remembered vaguely an order for twelve such ships as the *Wotan* had originally been designed to be, remembered it because the newspapers had hailed the order as a proof of post-war recovery, expansion, and prosperity.

He wondered if all twelve of those rockets were actually operating on the run for which they had supposedly been purchased.

"That is the trouble with you stupid Americans," von Hartwick went on. "You assume that every one shares your silly belief in such rotten things as democracy. But it is not true. We have friends everywhere. Even in Washington, in London, yes, even in Moscow. Our friends are everywhere. That is another reason why we will win."

"Even in New Mexico, maybe?"

Von Hartwick laughed. "That was a droll comedy, my friend. I enjoyed the daily reports. It would not have suited us to frighten you too much, until it began to appear that you might be successful. You were very lucky, my friend, that you took off as soon as you did."

"Don't call me 'my friend,' " Cargraves said testily. "I'm sick of it."

"Very well, my dear Captain." Cargraves let the remark pass. He was getting worried by the extended absence of Art and Morrie. Was it possible that some other of the Nazis were still around, alive and capable of making trouble?

He was beginning to think about tying up the prisoner here present and going to look for them when the lock sighed open. Morrie and Art stepped out, prodding the other prisoner before them. "He didn't want to come, Uncle," Art informed him. "We had to convince him a little." He chuckled. "I don't think he trusts us."

"Okay. Get your suits off."

The other prisoner seemed completely dumfounded by the sight of von Hartwick. Hastily he unclamped his helmet, threw it back, and said in German, "*Herr Oberst*—it was not my fault. I was——"

"Silence!" shouted the Nazi officer, also in German. "Have you told these pig-dogs anything about the operation of this ship?"

"*Nein, nein, Herr Oberst*—I swear it!"

"Then play stupid or I'll cut your heart out!"

Cargraves listened to this interesting little exchange with an expressionless face, but it was too much for Art. "Uncle," he demanded, "did you hear that? Did you hear what he said he'd do?"

Von Hartwick looked from nephew to uncle. "So you understand German?" he said quietly. "I was afraid that you might."

Ross had let the muzzle of his gun wander away from von Hartwick when the boys came in with their prisoner. Cargraves had long since shoved the pistol he had appropriated into his belt.

Von Hartwick glanced from one to another. Morrie and Art were both armed, one with a Garand, the other with revolver, but they had them trained on the Nazi pilot. Von Hartwick lunged suddenly at Cargraves and snatched the pistol from his belt.

Without appearing to stop to take aim he fired once. Then Cargraves was at him, clawing at his hands.

Von Hartwick brought the pistol down on his head, club fashion, and moved in to grapple him about the waist.

The Nazi pilot clasped his hands to his chest, gave a single bubbly moan, and sank to the floor. No one paid him any attention. After a split second of startled inaction, the three boys were milling around, trying to get in a shot at von Hartwick without hitting Cargraves. Cargraves himself had jerked and gone limp when the barrel of the pistol struck his head. Von Hartwick held the doctor's thirty pounds of moon-weight up with one arm. He shouted, "Silence!"

His order would have had no effect had not the boys seen something else: Von Hartwick was holding the pistol to Cargraves' head. "Careful, gentlemen," he said, speaking very rapidly. "I have no wish to harm your leader and will not do so unless you force me. I am sorry I was forced to strike him; I was forced to do so when he attacked me."

"Watch out!" commanded Morrie. "Art! Ross! Don't try to shoot."

"That is sensible," von Hartwick commended him. "I have no wish to try to shoot it out with you. My only purpose was to dispose of *him*." He indicated the body of the Nazi pilot.

Morrie glanced at it. "Why?"

"He was a soft and foolish pig. I could not afford to risk his courage. He would have told you what you want to know." He paused, and then said suddenly, "And now—I am your prisoner again!" The pistol sailed out of his hand and clanged against the floor.

"Get Doc out of my way," Ross snapped. "I can't get a shot in."

"No!" Morrie thundered. "Art, pick up the pistol. Ross, you take care of Doc."

"What are you talking about?" Ross objected. "He's a killer. I'll finish him off."

"No!"

"Why not?"

"Well—Doc wouldn't like it. That's reason enough. Don't shoot. That's an order, Ross. You take care of Doc. Art, you tie up the mug. Make it good."

"It'll be good!" promised Art.

The Nazi did not resist and Morrie found himself able to give some attention to what Ross was doing. "How bad is it?" he inquired, bending over Cargraves.

"Not too bad, I think. I'll know better when I get some of this blood wiped away."

"You will find dressings and such things," von Hartwick put in casually, as if he were not in the stages of being tied up, "in a kit under the instrument board in the control room."

"Go look for them, Ross," Morrie directed. "I'll keep guard. Not," he said to von Hartwick, "that it will do you any good if he dies. If he does, out you go, outside, without a suit. Shooting's too good for you."

"He won't die. I hit him very carefully."

"You had better hope he doesn't. You won't outlive him more than a couple of minutes."

Von Hartwick shrugged. "It is hardly possible to threaten me. We are all dead men. You realize that, don't you?"

Morrie looked at him speculatively. "Finished with him, Art? Sure he's tied up tight?"

"He'll choke himself to death if he tries to wiggle out of that one."

"Good. Now you," he went on to von Hartwick, "you may be a dead man. I wouldn't know. But we're not. We are going to fly this ship back to earth. You start behaving yourself and we might take you with us."

Von Hartwick laughed. "Sorry to disillusion you, dear boy, but none of us is going back to earth. That is why I had to dispose of that precious pilot of mine."

Morrie turned away, suddenly aware that no one had bothered to find out how badly the sergeant-pilot was wounded. He was soon certain; the man was dead, shot through the heart. "I can't see that it matters," he told von Hartwick. "We've still got you. You'll talk, or I'll cut your ears off and feed them to you."

"What a distressing thought," he was answered, "but it won't help you. You see, I am unable to tell you anything; I am not a pilot."

Art stared at him. "He's kidding you, Morrie."

"No," von Hartwick denied. "I am not. Try cutting my ears off and you will see. No, my poor boys, we are all going to stay here a long time, until we rot, in fact. *Heil dem Führer!*"

"Don't touch him, Art," Morrie warned. "Doc wouldn't like it."

XVIII TOO LITTLE TIME

CARGRAVES WAS WIDE ENOUGH awake to swear by the time Ross swabbed germicide on the cut in his hair line. "Hold still, Doc!"

"I am holding still. Take it easy."

They brought him up to date as they bandaged him. "The stinker thinks he's put one over on us," Ross finished. "He thinks we can't run this boat without somebody to show us."

"He may be perfectly right," Cargraves admitted. "So far it's got us stumped. We'll see. Throw him in the hold, and we'll have another look. Morrie, you did right not to let him be shot."

"I didn't think you would want him killed until you had squeezed him dry."

Cargraves gave him an odd smile. "That wasn't your only reason, was it?"

"Well—shucks!" Morrie seemed almost embarrassed. "I didn't want to just shoot him down after he dropped the gat. That's a Nazi trick."

Cargraves nodded approvingly. "That's right. That's one of the reasons they think we are soft. But we'll have a little surprise for him." He got up, went over, and stirred von Hartwick with his toe. "Listen to me, you. If possible, I am going to take you back to earth to stand trial. If not, we'll try you here."

Von Hartwick lifted his eyebrows. "For making war on you? How delightfully American!"

"No, not for making war. There isn't any war, and there hasn't been any war. The Third Reich disappeared forever in the spring of 1945 and today there is peace between Germany and the United States, no matter how many pipsqueak gangsters may still be hiding out. No, you phony superman, you are going to be tried for the murder of your accomplice—that poor dupe lying over there." He turned away. "Chuck him in the hold, boys. Come on, Ross."

Three hours later Cargraves was quite willing to admit that von Hartwick was correct when he said that the operation of the *Wotan* could not be figured out by a stranger. There were strange controls on the arms of the piloting seats which certainly had to be the flight controls, but no matter what they twisted, turned or moved, nothing happened. And the drive itself was sealed away behind a bulkhead which, from the sound it gave off when pounded, was inches thick.

Cargraves doubted whether he could cut through even with a steel-cutting flame. He was very reluctant to attempt to do so in any case; an effort to solve the mysteries of the ship by such surgery might, as likely as not, result in disabling the ship beyond any hope of repairing it.

There should be an operation manual somewhere. They all searched for it. They opened anything that would open, crawled under anything that could be crawled under, lifted everything that would move. There was no control manual in the ship.

The search disclosed something else. There was no food in the ship. This latter point was becoming important.

"That's enough, sports," he announced when he was certain that further search would be useless. "We'll try their barracks next. We'll find it. Not to mention food. You come with me, Morrie, and pick out some groceries."

"Me too!" Art shouted. "I'll get some pictures. The moon people! Oh, boy!"

Cargraves wished regretfully that he were still young enough for it to be impossible to stay worried. "Well, all right," he agreed, "but where is your camera?"

Art's face fell. "It's in the Dog House," he admitted.

"I guess the pictures will have to wait. But come along; there is more electronic equipment down there than you can run and jump over. Maybe raising earth by radio will turn out to be easy."

"Why don't we all go?" Ross wanted to know. "*I* found the ruins, but I haven't had a chance to look at them."

"Sorry, Ross, but you've got to stay behind and stand guard over Stinky. He might know more about this ship than he admits. I would hate to come up that staircase and find the ship missing. Stand guard over him. Tell him that if he moves a muscle you'll slug him. And mean it."

"Okay. I hope he does move. How long will you be gone?"

"If we can't find it in two hours we'll come back."

Cargraves searched the officers' room first, as it seemed the most likely place. He did not find it, but he did find that some of the Nazis appeared to have some peculiar and unpleasant tastes in books and pictures. The barrack room he took next. It was as depressing a place as it had been earlier, but he was prepared for it. Art he had assigned to the radio-and-radar room and Morrie to the other spaces; there seemed to be no reason for any one but himself to have to touch the bloating corpses.

He drew a blank in the barrack room. Coming out, he heard Art's voice in his phones. "Hey, Uncle, look what I've found!"

"What is it?" he said, and Morrie's voice cut in at once, "Found the manual, Art?"

"No, but look!" They converged in the central hall. "It" was a Graflex camera, complete with flash gun. "There is a complete darkroom off the radio room. I found it there. How about it, Uncle? Pictures?"

"Well, all right. Morrie, you go along—it may be your only chance to see the ruins. Thirty minutes. Don't go very far, don't bust your necks, don't take any chances, and be back on time, or I'll be after you with a Flit gun." He watched them go regretfully, more than a little tempted to play hookey himself. If he had not been consumed with the urgency of his present responsibilities——

But he was. He forced himself to resume the dreary search.

It was all to no good. If there was an instructional manual in existence he had to admit that he did not know how to find it. But he was still searching when the boys returned.

He glanced at his watch. "Forty minutes," he said. "That's more prompt than I thought you would be; I expected to have to go look for you. What did you find? Get any good pictures?"

"Pictures? Did we get pictures! Wait till you see!"

"I never saw anything like it, Doc," Morrie stated impressively. "The place is a city. It goes down and down. Great big arched halls, hundreds of feet across, corridors running every which way, rooms, balconies—I can't begin to describe it."

"Then don't try. Write up full notes on what you saw as soon as we get back."

"Doc, this thing's tremendous!"

"I realize it. But it's so big I'm not even going to try to comprehend it, not yet. We've got our work cut out for us just to get out of here alive. Art, what did you find in the radio room? Anything you can use to raise earth?"

"Well, Uncle, that's hard to say, but the stuff doesn't look promising."

"Are you sure? We know that they were in communication—at least according to our nasty-nice boy friend."

Art shook his head. "I thought you said they *received* from earth. I found their equipment for that but I couldn't test it out because I couldn't get the earphones inside my suit. But I don't see how they could *send* to earth."

"Why not? They need two-way transmission."

"Maybe they need it but they can't afford to use it. Look, Uncle, they can beam towards the moon from their base on earth—that's all right; nobody gets it but them. But if the Nazis on this end try to beam back, they can't select some exact spot on earth. At that distance the beam would fan out until it covered too much territory—it would be like a broadcast."

"Oh!" said Cargraves, "I begin to see. Chalk up one for yourself, Art; I should have thought of that. No matter what sort of a code they used, if people started picking up radio from the direction of the moon, the cat would be out of the bag."

"That's what I thought, anyhow."

"I think you're dead right. I'm disappointed; I was beginning to pin my hopes on getting a message across." He shrugged. "Well, one thing at a time. Morrie, have you picked out the supplies you want to take up?"

"All lined up." They followed him into the kitchen space and found he had stacked three piles of tin cans in quantities to make three good-sized loads. As they were filling their arms Morrie said. "How many men were here, Doc?"

"I counted forty-seven bodies not counting the one von Hartwick shot. Why?"

"Well, I noticed something funny. I've sort of acquired an eye for estimating rations since I've been running the mess. There isn't food enough here to keep that many men running two weeks. Does that mean what I think it means?"

"Hunnh . . . Look, Morrie, I think you've hit on something important. That's why von Hartwick is so cocky. It isn't just whistling in the dark. He actually expects to be rescued."

"What do you mean, Uncle?" Art wanted to know.

"He is expecting a supply ship, almost any time."

Art whistled. "He thinks we'll be caught by surprise!"

"And we would have been. But we won't be now." He put down his load of groceries. "Come along."

"Where?"

"I just remembered something." In digging through the officers' quarters he had come across many documents, books, manuals, records, and papers of many sorts. He had scanned them very briefly, making certain only that no one of them contained anything which would give a clue to the operation of the *Wotan*.

One of them was the day book or journal of the task-force commander. Among other things it had given the location of the Nazi base on earth; Cargraves had marked it as something he wanted to study later. Now he decided to do it at once.

It was long. It covered a period of nearly three months with Teutonic thoroughness. He read rapidly, with Art reading over his shoulder. Morrie stood around impatiently and finally pointed out that the time was approaching when they had promised Ross to return.

"Go ahead," Cargraves said absently. "Take a load of food. Get a meal started." He read on.

There was a roster of the party. He found von Hartwick listed as executive officer. He noted that as an indication that the Nazi was lying when he claimed not to understand the piloting of the *Wotan*. Not proof, but a strong indication. But falsehood was all that he expected of the creature.

He was beginning to find what he was looking for. Supply trips had been made each month. If the schedule was maintained—and the state of supplies certainly indicated it—the next ship should be along in six or seven days.

But the most important fact he was not sure of until he had finished the journal: there was more than one big rocket in their possession; the *Wotan* was not about to leave to get supplies; she would not leave, if the schedule had been followed, until the supply ship landed. Then she would be taken back empty and the other ship would be unloaded. By such an arrangement the party on the moon was never left without a means of escape—or, at least, that was the reason he read into the account.

There were just two and only two Nazi moon rockets—the *Wotan* and the *Thor*. The *Thor* was due in a week, as nearly as he could make out, which meant that she would leave her home base in about five days. The transit times for each trip had been logged in; forty-six hours plus for the earth-moon jump was the way the record read.

Fast time! he thought.

If the *Thor* ever took off, it might be too late for good intentions, too late for warnings. The Nazis were certainly aware that the techniques of space flight were now an open secret; there was reference after reference to the *Galileo* including a last entry noting that she had been located. They would certainly strike at the earliest possible moment.

He could see in his mind's eye the row upon row of A-bomb guided-missiles in a near-by cavern. He could see them striking the defenseless cities of earth.

No time to rig a powerful transmitter. No time for anything but drastic measures.

Not time enough, he was afraid!

XIX   SQUEEZE PLAY

"Soup's on!" Morrie greeted him as he came hurrying into the *Wotan*. Cargraves started shucking off his suit as he answered.

"No time for that—no, gimme a couple of those sandwiches."

Morrie complied. Ross inquired, "What's the rush?"

"Got to see the prisoner." He turned away, then stopped. "No—wait. Come here, guys." He motioned them into a football huddle. "I'm going to try something." He whispered urgently for a few minutes. "Now play up. I'll leave the door open."

He went into the hold and prodded von Hartwick with his boot. "Wake up, you." He took a bite of sandwich.

"I am awake." Von Hartwick turned his head with some difficulty as he was trussed up with his ankles pulled up toward his wrists, which were tied behind him. "Ah, food," he said cheerfully. "I was wondering when you would remember the amenities in dealing with prisoners."

"It's not for you," Cargraves informed him. "The other sandwich is for me. You won't need one."

Von Hartwick looked interested but not frightened. "So?"

"Nope," said Cargraves, wiping his mouth with his sleeve, "you won't. I had intended to take you to earth for trial, but I find I won't have time for that. I'll try you myself—now."

Von Hartwick shrugged under his bonds. "You are able to do as you like. I've no doubt you intend to kill me, but don't dignify it with the name of a trial. Call it a lynching. Be honest with yourself. In the first place my conduct has been entirely correct. True, I was forced to shoot one of my own men, but it was a necessary emergency military measure——"

"Murder," put in Cargraves.

"—in defense of the security of the Reich," von Hartwick went on unhurriedly, "and no concern of yours in any case. It was my own ship, entirely out of jurisdiction of any silly laws of the corrupt democracies. As for the bombing of your ship, I have explained to you——"

"Shut up," Cargraves said. "You'll get a chance to say a few words later. Court's in session. Just to get it straight in your head, this entire planet is subject to the laws of the United Nations. We took formal possession and have established a permanent base. Therefore——"

"Too late, Judge Lynch. The New Reich claimed this planet three months ago."

"I told you to keep quiet. You're in contempt of court. One more peep and we'll think up a way to keep you quiet. Therefore, as the master of a vessel registered under the laws of the United Nations it is my duty to see that those laws are obeyed. Your so-called claim doesn't hold water. There isn't any New Reich, so it can't claim anything. You and your fellow thugs aren't a nation; you are merely gangsters. We aren't bound to recognize any fictions you have thought up and we don't. Morrie! Bring me another sandwich."

"Coming up, Captain!"

"Now as master of the *Galileo*," Cargraves went on, "I have to act for the government when I'm off by myself, as I am now. Since I haven't time to take you back to earth for trial, I'm trying you now. Two charges: murder in the first degree and piracy."

"Piracy? My dear fellow!"

"Piracy. You attacked a vessel of UN register. On your own admission you took part in it, whether you gave the orders or not. All members of a pirate crew are equally guilty, and it's a capital offense. Murder in the first degree is another one. Thanks for the sandwich, Morrie. Where did you find fresh bread?"

"It was canned."

"Clever, these Nazis. There was some doubt in my mind as to whether to charge you with first or second degree. But you had to grab the gun away from me first, before you could shoot your pal. That's premeditation. So you're charged—piracy and first-degree murder. How do you plead? Guilty or not guilty?"

Von Hartwick hesitated a bit before replying. "Since I do not admit the jurisdiction of this so-called court, I refuse to enter a plea. Even if I concede—which I don't—that you honestly believe this to be United Nations territory, you still are not a court."

"A ship's master has very broad powers in an emergency. Look it up some time. Get a ouija board and look it up."

Von Hartwick raised his eyebrows. "From the nature of that supposedly humorous remark I can see that I am convicted before the trial starts."

Cargraves chewed reflectively. "In a manner of speaking, yes," he conceded. "I'd like to give you a jury, but we don't really need one. You see, there aren't any facts to be established because there aren't any facts in doubt. We were all there. The only question is: What do those facts constitute under the law? This is your chance to speak your piece if you intend to."

"Why should I bother? You mongrel nations prate of justice and equality under the law. But you don't practice it. You stand there with your hands dripping with the blood of my comrades, whom you killed in cold blood, without giving them a chance—yet you speak to me of piracy and murder!"

"We discussed that once before," Cargraves answered carefully. "There is a world of difference, under the laws of free men, between an unprovoked attack and striking back in your own defense. If a footpad assaults you in a dark alley, you don't have to get a court order to fight back. Next. Got any more phony excuses?"

The Nazi was silent. "Go ahead," Cargraves persisted. "You could still plead not guilty by reason of insanity and you might even convince me. I always have thought a man with a Master-Race complex was crazy as a hoot owl. You might convince me that you were crazy in a legal sense as well."

For the first time, von Hartwick's air of aloof superiority seemed to crack. His face got red and he appeared about to explode. Finally he regained a measure of control and said, "Let's have no more of this farce. Do whatever it is you intend to do and quit playing with me."

"I assure you that I am not playing. Have you anything more to say in your own defense?"

"No!"

"I find you guilty on both charges. Have you anything to say before sentence is passed?"

The accused did not deign to answer.

"Very well. I sentence you to death."

Art took a quick, gasping breath and backed out of the doorway where he had been huddled, wide-eyed, with Ross and Morrie. There was no other sound.

"Have you anything to say before the sentence executed?"

Von Hartwick turned his face away. "I am not sorry. At least I will have a quick and merciful death. The best you four swine can hope for is a slow and lingering death."

"Oh," said Cargraves, "I intended to explain to you about that. We aren't going to die."

"You think not?" There was undisguised triumph in von Hartwick's voice.

"I'm sure of it. You see, the *Thor* arrives in six or seven days——"

"*What?* How did you find that out?" The Nazi seemed stunned for a moment, then muttered, "Not that it matters . . . four of you—but I see why you decided to kill me. You were afraid I would escape you."

"Not at all," returned Cargraves. "You don't understand. If it were practical to do so, I would take you back to earth to let you appeal your case before a higher court. Not for your sake—you're guilty as sin!—but for my own. However, I do not find it possible. We will be very busy until the *Thor* gets here and I have no means of making sure that you are securely imprisoned except by standing guard over you every minute. I can't do that; we haven't time enough. But I don't intend to let you escape punishment. I don't have a cell to put you in. I had intended to drain the fuel from your little rocket and put you in there, without a suit. That way, you would have been safe to leave alone while we worked. But, now that the *Thor* is coming, we will need the little rocket."

Von Hartwick smiled grimly. "Think you can run away, eh? That ship will never take you home. Or haven't you found that out yet?"

"You still don't understand. Keep quiet and let me explain. We are going to take several of the bombs such as you used on the *Galileo* and blow up the room containing your guided missiles. It's a shame, for I see it's one of the rooms built by the original inhabitants. Then we are going to blow up the *Wotan.*"

"The *Wotan?* Why?" Von Hartwick was suddenly very alert.

"To make sure it never flies back to earth. We can't operate it; I must make sure that no one else does. For then we intend to blow up the *Thor.*"

"The *Thor?* You can't blow up the *Thor!*"

"Oh, yes, we can—the same way you blew up the *Galileo.* But I can't chance the possibility of survivors grabbing the *Wotan*—so she must go first. And that has a strong bearing

181

on why you must die at once. After we blast the *Wotan* we are going back to our own base—you didn't know about that, did you?—but it is only one room. No place for prisoners. I had intended, as I said, to keep you in the jeep rocket, but the need to blast the *Thor* changes that. We'll have to keep a pilot in it all times, until the *Thor* lands. And that leaves no place for you. Sorry," he finished, and smiled.

"Anything wrong with it?" he added.

Von Hartwick was beginning to show the strain. "You may succeed——"

"Oh, we will!"

"But if you do, you are still dead men. A quick death for me, but a long and slow and lingering death for you. If you blast the *Thor*, you lose your own last chance. Think of it," he went on, "starving or suffocating or dying with cold. I'll make a pact with you. Turn me loose now and I'll give you my parole. When the *Thor* arrives, I'll intercede with the captain on your behalf. I'll——"

Cargraves cut him off with a gesture. "The word of a Nazi! You wouldn't intercede for your own grandmother! You haven't gotten it through your thick head yet that we hold all the aces. After we kill you and take care of your friends, we shall sit tidy and cozy and warm, with plenty of food and air, until we are picked up. We won't even be lonesome; we were just finishing our earth sender when you picked up one of our local signals. We'll——"

"You lie!" shouted von Hartwick. "No one will pick you up. Yours was the only ship. I know, I know. We had full reports."

"*Was* the only ship." Cargraves smiled sweetly. "But under a quaint old democratic law which you wouldn't understand, the plans and drawings and notes for my ship were being studied eagerly the minute we took off. We'll be able to take our pick of ships before long. I hate to disappoint you on another score. Your death will not be as clean and pleasant as you had hoped."

"What do you mean?"

"I mean I am not going to get this ship all bloodied up again by shooting you. I'm going to——"

"Wait. A dying man is entitled to a last request. Leave me in the *Wotan*. Let me die with my ship!"

Cargraves laughed full in his face. "Lovely, von Nitwit. Perfectly lovely. And have you take off in her. Not likely!"

"I am no pilot—believe me!"

"Oh, I do believe. I would not think of doubting a dying man's last words. But I won't risk a mistake. Ross!"

"Yes, sir!"

"Take this thing and throw it out on the face of the moon."

"Dee-lighted!"

"And that's all." Cargraves had been squatting down; he got up and brushed the crumbs from his hands. "I shan't even have you untied so that you can die in a comfortable position. You are too handy at grabbing guns. You'll just have to flop around as you are. It probably won't take long," he went on conversationally. "They say it's about like drowning. In seven or eight minutes you won't know a thing. Unless your heart ruptures through your lungs and finishes you a little sooner."

"Swine!"

"*Captain* Swine, to you."

Ross was busily zipping his suit into place. "Okay, Doc?"

"Go ahead. No, on second thought," he added, "I'll do this job myself. I might be criticized for letting a boy touch it. My suit, Morrie."

He whistled as they helped him dress. He was still whistling as he picked up von Hartwick like a satchel, by the line which bound his ankles to his wrists, and walked briskly to the lock. He chucked his bundle in ahead of him, stepped in, waved to the boy, said, "Back soon!" and clamped the door.

As the air started whistling out von Hartwick began to gasp. Cargraves smiled at him, and said, "Drafty, isn't it?" He shouted to make himself heard through the helmet.

Von Hartwick's mouth worked.

"Did you say something?"

The Nazi opened his mouth again, gasped, choked, and sprayed foam out on his chest. "You'll have to talk louder," Cargraves shouted. "I can't hear you." The air whistled away.

"*I'm a pilot!*"

"What?"

"*I'm a pilot! I'll teach you——*"

Cargraves reached up and closed the exhaust valve. "I can't hear with all that racket. What were you saying?"

"I'm a pilot!" gasped von Hartwick.

"Yes? Well, what about it?"

"Air. Give me air——"

"Shucks," said Cargraves. "You've got plenty of air. I can still hear you talking. Must be four or five pounds in here."

"Give me air. I'll tell you how it works."

"You'll tell me *first*," Cargraves stated. He reached for the exhaust valve again.

"Wait! There is a little plug, in the back of the instrument—" He paused and gasped heavily. "The instrument panel. Starboard side. It's a safety switch. You wouldn't notice it; it looks just like a mounting stud. You push it in." He stopped to wheeze again.

"I think you'd better come show me," Cargraves said judicially. "If you aren't lying again, you've given me an out to take you back to earth for your appeal. Not that you deserve it."

He reached over and yanked on the spill valve; the air rushed back into the lock.

Ten minutes later Cargraves was seated in the left-hand pilot's chair, with his safety belt in place. Von Hartwick was in the right-hand chair. Cargraves held a pistol in his left hand and cradled it over the crook of his right arm, so that it would remain pointed at von Hartwick, even under drive.

"Morrie! Everybody ready?"

"Ready, Captain," came faintly from the rear of the ship. The boys had been forced to use the acceleration bunks in the passenger compartment. They resented it, especially

Morrie, but there was no help for it. The control room could carry just two people under acceleration.

"Okay! Here we go!" He turned again to von Hartwick. "Twist her tail, Swine—Colonel Swine, I mean."

Von Hartwick glared at him. "I don't believe," he said slowly, "that you ever intended to go through with it."

Cargraves grinned and rubbed the chair arm. "Want to go back and see?" he inquired.

Von Hartwick swiveled his head around to the front. "*Achtung!*" he shouted. "Prepare for acceleration! Ready—" Without waiting for a reply he blasted off.

The ship had power to spare with the light load; Cargraves had him hold it at two *g*'s for five minutes and then go free. By that time, having accelerated at nearly 64 feet per second for each second of the five minutes, even with due allowance for loss of one-sixth *g* to the pull of the moon at the start, they were making approximately 12,000 miles per hour.

They would have breezed past earth in twenty hours had it not been necessary to slow down in order to land. Cargraves planned to do it in a little less than twenty-four hours.

Once in free fall, the boys came forward and Cargraves required of von Hartwick a detailed lecture on the operation of the craft. When he was satisfied, he said, "Okay. Ross, you and Art take the prisoner aft and lash him to one of the bunks. Then strap yourselves down. Morrie and I are going to practice."

Von Hartwick started to protest. Cargraves cut him short. "Stow it! You haven't been granted any pardon; we've simply been picking your brains. You are a common criminal, going back to appeal your case."

They felt out the ship for the next several hours, with time only to eat. The result of the practice on the course and speed were null; careful check was kept by instrument to see that a drive in one direction was offset by the same amount of drive in the opposite direction. Then they slept.

They needed sleep. By the time they got it they had been

awake and active at an unrelenting pace for one full earth-day.

When they woke Cargraves called Art. "Think you could raise earth on this Nazi gear, kid?"

"I'll try. What do you want me to say and who do you want to talk to?"

Cargraves considered. Earth shone gibbous, more than half full, ahead. The Nazi base was not in line-of-sight. That suited him. "Better make it Melbourne, Australia," he decided, "and tell them this——"

Art nodded. A few minutes later, having gotten the hang of the strange set, he was saying endlessly: "Space Ship *City of Detroit* calling UN police patrol, Melbourne; Space Ship *City of Detroit* calling UN police patrol, Melbourne——"

He had been doing this for twenty-five minutes when a querulous voice answered: "Pax, Melbourne; Pax, Melbourne —calling Space Ship *City of Detroit*. Come in, *City of Detroit.*"

Art pushed up one phone and looked helpless. "You better talk to 'em, Uncle."

"Go ahead. You tell them what I told you. It's your show." Art shut up and did so.

Morrie let her down carefully and eased her over into a tight circular orbit just outside the atmosphere. Their speed was still nearly five miles per second; they circled the globe in ninety minutes. From that orbit he killed her speed slowly and dipped down cautiously until the stub wings of the *City of Detroit* né *Wotan*, began to bite the tenuous stratosphere in a blood-chilling thin scream.

Out into space again they went and then back in, each time deeper and each time slower. On the second of the braking orbits they heard the broadcast report of the UN patrol raid on the Nazi nest and of the capture of the *Thor*. On the next lap two chains bid competitively for an exclusive broadcast from space. On the third there was dickering for television rights at the field. On the fourth they received official instructions to attempt to land at the District-of-Columbia Rocket Port.

"Want me to take her down?" Morrie yelled above the scream of the skin friction.

"Go right ahead," Cargraves assured him. "I'm an old man. I want a chauffeur."

Morrie nodded and began his approach. They were somewhere over Kansas.

The ground of the rocket port felt strange and solid under the ship. Eleven days—only eleven days?—away from the earth's massive pull had given them new habits. Cargraves found that he staggered a little in trying to walk. He opened the inner door of the lock and waited for the boys to get beside him. Latching the inner door open, he stepped to the outer door and broke the seal.

As he swung it open, a solid wall of sound beat him in the face, an endless mass of eager eyes looked up at him. Flash guns flickered like heat lightning. He turned back to Ross. "Oh, my gosh!" he said. "This is awful! Say—don't you guys want to take the bows?"